# My Teacher's a Bug

# SPINETINGLERS

## #3

# My Teacher's a Bug

# M. T. COFFIN

AN AVON CAMELOT BOOK

MY TEACHER'S A BUG is an original publication of Avon Books. This work has never before appeared in book form.

AVON BOOKS
A division of
The Hearst Corporation
1350 Avenue of the Americas
New York, New York 10019

Copyright © 1995 by Robert Hawks
Excerpt from *Where Have All The Parents Gone?* copyright © 1995 by George Edward Stanley
Published by arrangement with the author
Library of Congress Catalog Card Number: 94-96710
ISBN: 0-380-77785-1
RL: 4.9

First Avon Camelot Printing: May 1995

CAMELOT TRADEMARK REG. U.S. PAT. OFF. AND IN OTHER COUNTRIES, MARCA REGISTRADA, HECHO EN U.S.A.

Printed in the U.S.A.

OPM   10   9   8   7   6   5   4   3   2   1

For Ruth, who never lets me down

# PROLOGUE

Before this story started, an article appeared in the *Weekly World Star,* one of those supermarket checkout counter newspapers. Almost nobody read it, but you should.

## AIRLINE PILOTS SEE MONSTER!

Three commercial airline pilots were recently suspended from flight duties after reporting that they saw a monster—a yellow-and-black gargoylelike winged beast—flying before them as they navigated at 37,000 feet over the southwestern United States.

Cockpit voice recorders backed up the tale of the aircrew of a TransGlobal Air flight as they described in awed voices the spectacle of seeing a horrifying, scale-covered beast wearing what appeared to be armor and carrying some sort of sword as their aircraft flew six miles above the earth. The monster was carrying something in a large bag—something alive—and he seemed furious upon being spotted by the aircrew, waving his sword and flying down, out of sight! All three pilots were immediately suspended by the airline upon landing and describing what they saw, but the captain of the airliner describes that he and his crew's "entire lives have changed" since the event. They are unable to sleep much of the time, unable to convince others of what they personally witnessed. "Monster, devil, demon? Is it the dark lord? Tell me! Could we have seen the dark lord himself?"

Who could say?

Indeed. Who could say?
I could, actually. But not right now. . . .

# I

# Some More Important Stuff Before the First Bug Bites

*Six times in history, six times in history,* the thought keeps running through your mind, an unwelcome singsong, and then you start to wonder if perhaps you're confused, getting it wrong. Maybe the thought is supposed to be six times to history, or history six times, or six times in math class, then you go on to history; it's that crazy a thing.

So you forget about it, and that's an easy enough thing, losing track, since you seem to have blanked out not only your own name but nearly everything else about your life.

Well, almost everything. You still remember you're thirteen, and what chocolate ice cream tastes like, and what sand feels like between your toes on the beach, and how you're allergic to mayonnaise. You know what it feels like to skid on your bike and fly off hard, skinning up your knees so they burn when they hit the bathwater and you remember being mad at your mother for something, but you can't remember what it is and that's scary, hating somebody for something you can't remember, especially when all of a sudden you couldn't pull your mother out of a lineup, but one more thing—very important—you do not, absolutely do not, believe in flying saucers. . . .

The man in black believed in flying saucers, but then again he believed in a lot of things, including Bigfoot, the Loch Ness monster, unicorns, the lost continent of Atlantis, and schoolteachers when they promised to never, ever give homework on Fridays.

Being the man in black, he was allowed to indulge in the occasional fantasy. Kids don't have that luxury, especially thirteen-year-old girls with amnesia, and the man in black was nowhere to be seen on that Friday afternoon when the girl was sitting at a picnic table out in front of the Teddle, Texas, Dairy Queen. She wasn't eating anything, just sitting quietly, contemplating an ant as it pulled itself across the length of the

cracked red plastic, dragging a speck of something, food. A crumb of bread, probably of hot dog
bun. The ant was having a difficult time of it.

A Texas state police car slid into the parking
lot, crackling gravel beneath its wheels as it
stopped and the cop got out, leaving his hat on
the seat, ambling casually. His name was Tony,
and he smiled at the girl. There was no one else
outside the Dairy Queen, as it was eight-thirty
in the morning and the DQ didn't actually open
until ten. "Hey," said Tony the cop. "How you
doing?"

The girl shrugged. A few days unwashed, her
hair fell heavily across her eyes, and she brushed
it back. Something about the movement startled
Tony the cop, but he didn't say anything, not
quite yet.

"Are you waiting for somebody?"

"Yes," she said.

"Anything I can do for you?"

The girl shook her head.

Tony the cop stood there a long moment, looking up and down the single street that repre-
sented nearly the entire town of Teddle. "You live
in town?" He knew that she didn't.

She shook her head.

"Are you from Clark?"

Clark was the nearest real city, small as it was,

about thirty-five miles up the road; that's where Tony lived.

The girl hesitated. "I don't think so."

Tony the cop frowned. "Who are you waiting for?"

"I don't know."

"You don't know?"

She shook her head again and for the first time seemed lost as opposed to just out of place: a small animal caught in a sudden flash of light.

In his kindest voice, Tony asked, "What's your name, honey?"

The girl considered this, thought about it a long moment, and Tony assumed she was inventing up a lie, a fake name to give him. A lot of kids did that, especially kids with problems at home. What she said, though, was, "I forget."

"You forget?"

She nodded, her eyes all of a sudden extraordinarily bright. "Yeah. I forget my name. Isn't that weird?"

"Yes," agreed Tony the cop. "It sure is weird. Do you have any ID? Anything with your picture or your name written on it?"

Another shake of the head. "No, I checked. Just as soon as I first realized I didn't have a name I looked to see if I had a purse, a wallet, but I don't. That's a weird thing to realize, to all of a sudden think, hey, I don't even know my own name."

"Yeah."

"I mean, I must have a name. It would be kind of hard getting around without one."

"Yeah."

"I guess it could be done, though."

"It would be hard. Where do you get around from?"

"Excuse me?"

Tony the cop prodded. "Where are you from? Do you remember that much?"

"No. It's really funny. I don't remember anything except walking. Up that road there. It was like waking up from a deep sleep, but doing it slowly, like I was a cat getting up from a nap, you know? And I'm awake now and I'm walking, and the town is here, and I'm sort of tired so I thought I'd sit down and rest."

"Yeah."

"That was a while ago, though. It was dark then. I've been here a while."

"Sitting?"

"Yeah."

"You said you were waiting for somebody."

"I sort of feel like I am, you know? Only I can't remember who."

"Maybe you should come with me."

The girl seemed to consider this. "Will you take me to jail?"

"Oh no, no way, not to jail. We can get you something to eat, see if we can figure out who you are."

The girl brightened. "That would be great."

"Come on, then."

She got up from the bench and followed Tony the cop over to his car. "You know," she said, the thought seeming to suddenly occur to her, "there really is such a thing as a cynget."

"A what?"

"A cynget. Sin-jet. There really is such a thing."

Tony the cop was curious. "What is a cynget?"

The girl's face was bright. "I don't know. Isn't that weird? I don't even know what a cynget is, but I know they exist."

"I'm sure they do."

A lot of people thought the man in black was a little goofy, wearing the same black suit all the time, but he was tolerated by the many government agencies he worked for since he was obviously involved with something important. Besides, he was usually gone. In fact, the man in black had been checking out the story behind the birth of a three-headed cow when the explosion ripped through the night sky over south Texas.

The man in black found the man in charge of the scene, the fire chief, over by one of the foam tanker trucks. His name was Green and he seemed a little unnerved by it all. "Nine hours," he said, awed. "We've been attacking this fire for almost nine hours and nothing.

"It's a big jet, but . . . we haven't found any bodies yet." The fire chief spoke a little hesitantly, like a gambler afraid to talk about a winning streak for fear of cursing it.

"Cargo jet," explained the man in black. "Lucky break. Mostly just overnight packages."

"Thank God for that."

"Bees, I think."

"Bees?"

"New kind of bees," said the man in black. "Special honey bees; they're bred to produce a lot more honey. They're . . . uh . . . bigger."

"Bigger bees?"

"A lot bigger."

The fire chief nodded. "We'll be able to figure things out better when we get the fire doused."

"Tell your men to be careful."

"We're always careful."

The man in black nodded and ambled over to the police line, where a pair of sheriff's deputies were watching the billowing flames. "How you guys doing?"

9

"Who are you?"

The man in black flashed one of his IDs, explaining, "Some of our cargo was on the plane, Department of Agriculture stuff. Bad luck."

"You sure got here fast."

"Fast? I'm lucky I wasn't on it. I was supposed to be."

"Really?" Now the cops were interested, and the man in black entertained them with a diverting story about his brush with death. As he spoke, neither cop seemed to notice how intently the man in black was scanning the wreckage.

He was looking for survivors. Unlikely, and probably for the best. Next he was hoping the thing would burn itself to ashes and then be blown away to the four winds. Also unlikely.

"What kind of cargo was it?" asked one of the cops now. "Can you say?"

The man in black did say, again, telling some of the truth and mostly lies, explaining about the experimental honey bees and how they were, well, bigger than most bees.

"Wow," said the cop, impressed. "Superbees. Wow. Where'd they come from?"

"Well, I can't exactly tell you," said the man in black. "It's sort of classified, you know?"

The cop grinned. "You could tell us, but then you'd have to kill us?"

It was the man in black's turn to grin, a fine and natural expression for his face. "I almost never kill anybody. . . ."

## 2

# SOUTH TEXAS

My name is Ryan Sullivan.

My family moved to south Texas because Dad—
Mr. Thomas Montgomery Sullivan—got a great job
there working on some sort of secret project at Teddle Base, a weird combined military installation
that took up most of the town. Being a defense
engineer, Dad was moved before, and we've been
around air force and navy bases, but this place was
different. It had navy, air force, and army guys
running about all over, but the town itself seemed
mostly empty. As always, Dad wasn't even allowed
to talk about it to us. "I'll tell you all this much,"
he did say before we moved. "This job pays more
money than it should—more money than we've
ever made—especially since there are fewer and
fewer jobs, even in California."

**12**

So we wound up in Teddle, Texas.

There was one real street in Teddle, with the town in the center and houses on both ends, and maybe six or seven other smaller streets criss-crossing this. There were a lot of empty houses in Teddle; not boarded up or anything, just abandoned. Dad said this was probably because of the defense cutbacks—a lot of the base was most likely shut down, meaning the workers had to move away.

Except it wasn't as if they had moved away. This was something that took a while to notice, but a lot of the abandoned houses still had furniture inside, toys idle on the lawns. It was as if the owners were only gone for a while, expecting to eventually return.

Only nobody ever went into the empty houses; there was a silence about some of those side streets that was like being caught alone in an alley, late on Halloween night, with nothing but blowing leaves for company. I know this for a fact, because if anyone had been going in and out of those houses, we would have known it, because Teddle was a screen-door town.

Let me explain that. Every house had a screen door, but more than that, every screen door opened at once whenever something happened. If the ice cream man drove through, twenty screen doors popped open. Should a kid laugh too loudly, or some driver squeal the brakes hard when pausing at one of the five stop signs in town, twenty screen doors would open.

Kids jabbered, mothers talked, fathers conversed. Things happened more slowly in south Texas, so there was more time to discuss them. Ma said it the second day we were there: "There are no secrets in Teddle."

She was never more wrong in her life.

As I said, though, Teddle, Texas, was mostly Teddle Base, Texas, with lots of chain-link fences blocking off parts of the desert and roads that led smack into gates where mean-looking marine guards seemed to be protecting nothing more than weeds and dirt and signs reading RE-STRICTED AREA—NO ENTRY—USE OF DEADLY FORCE IS AUTHORIZED. Which meant, Dad said, that they could shoot you.

I wasn't worried about being shot dead by some guard, though. Guards and guns weren't my problem. Aside from boredom, the climate was the only thing that was killing me—well, not exactly killing me—but it wasn't any fun.

Allergies. All of a sudden I had horrible allergies to something, some kind of pollen or whatever in the air, and it got to where I woke up

**14**

every morning stuffed up, congested, and blasting a few sneezes.

"Sheesh, hack it up, bud," said Anthony, my older brother, as I sat down to the breakfast table the last free Friday morning before school started again.

"Sheesh," said Anthony again. He was fifteen and going on nine. "Blow your nose or something. And don't make that honking noise, either; that makes me sick to my stomach. I can't even eat my eggs."

"Nobody could eat your eggs," I said, reaching for the box of tissues on the kitchen counter. Lately Anthony had decided not only was he supposedly this great bike rider—the King of all Wheelies he called himself—but he could also cook better than Ma, so he made his own eggs in the morning. As always they were grotesque runny things that a goat couldn't choke down, but Anthony savored them as if a French chef had slaved for hours.

"Where's the real food?" I asked, reaching over to switch on the radio. Weird Wally was on, the wild disc jockey at KTED, the local station. Sometimes he was rude, but I thought he was funny.

"Eggs or frozen waffles," answered Ma, reaching to switch off the radio. She thought Weird Wally was rude but almost never funny.

"Waffles," I decided instantly. "Who can even think about eggs after watching the King of all Wimpies experiment with them?"

"Look who's calling who a wimpie, sneeze-face. Aim it somewhere else, would you?"

"Enough," said Ma, passing me a plate with two toaster-browned waffles. "We are going to have to get you over to the doctor about these allergies."

"A shot!" cried Anthony, almost giggling with delight. "A shot! A shot! A shot!"

"Big deal," I said, not letting him get to me. "I'm not afraid of shots. Let him give me ten shots." Which was sort of a bluff, I guess. I'm not one of those people with horrible fears of shots, but ten whacks with a needle would give anybody the willies.

"You may not even need a shot," said Ma, playing the role of concerned parent trying to keep her kid from freaking out and breaking for the door. "Probably just some hyped-up cold medicine, but we'll see. They fit you in for an appointment tomorrow morning."

"On Saturday? Ma, come on. . . ."

"When else? It's got to be taken care of now, before school, which is Monday. You don't want to be sneezing all over people the first day of school, do you?"

"Yeah, but . . ."

"Not buts. Plan on it."

"Whatever," I said.

Then I sneezed.

So Ma took me to the doctor, an allergy guy who seemed unconcerned as he scratched my arm with a needle and finally gave me a shot and prescribed some pills.

"There could be some mild side effects," he warned me and Ma.

Mild side effects.

If only he'd known. Maybe he still would have given me the shot, maybe he wouldn't have. See, to this day I still don't know whether that allergy guy was a human or not. . . .

## 3

# WEIRD WALLY

Monday was the first day of school, but—and I know this sounds like a TV commercial break only it isn't—first a word about the man in black.

Ever read about flying saucers or UFOs or the Bermuda Triangle or any of that scary stuff? I used to; it's nothing you could call a hobby, but it's cool stuff to read—visitors from outer space, strange, unexplained disappearances out on the ocean. Whole ships and planes have vanished like a puff of smoke, and nobody knows how or why.

Nobody except maybe the man in black.

Read the serious stuff about flying saucers: the weird, serious stuff, and there's always the same story, again and again. Some yahoo gets kidnapped by a flying saucer, and they take him to Jupiter or whatever to test his IQ and discover

**18**

he's got the intellect of an artichoke—or at least that's what he tells the *Weekly World News* when he sells his story for a couple of thousand dollars. And usually he's lying, just some goof who figures what the heck, telling tall tales is an American tradition going back to Paul Bunyan and Davy Crockett; why not make a buck?

Except this person always gets a visit from the man in black.

And the man in black never knows which stories are real, which are nonsense, not until he goes and checks them out for himself.

Which he does. Every one of them, no matter how loony, because loony is as loony does, and if the Great Chicago fire really got started by an old lady's cow kicking over a lantern, then anything is possible, right?

So says the man in black.

And I'm assuming there's only one man in black, the one I met, but that might not be true, either. Maybe there's a bunch of them, a dozen, maybe even an army of men in black, all out there in their black cars, with their backseats full of crumpled supermarket tabloids and their radio stations tuned to the weirdest points on the dial they can find, all with the idea that even if only one in a thousand weird stories is true, then

**19**

there's still a lot of truly strange stuff out there that must be checked up on.

Thank goodness for that, folks, because me and the man in black saved the world, although I hold him partly to blame, too, since he's the one who tried to destroy it in the first place. . . .

As I said, though, the first day of school—first morning of the first day, actually—my brother and I were eating in the kitchen, listening to Weird Wally on the radio talking to a lady who said she knew something about cyngets.

"What, may I ask," said Weird Wally as only he can, "are you talking about? What's a cynget? Why should I care?"

The lady's voice dropped off to a whisper. "It's sort of a flying saucer."

"Of course it is," said Weird Wally as my brother winged a piece of raisin toast at me. I cranked the radio a little louder: "And have you been zipping around much lately on these flying saucers? To Mars, maybe? To Jupiter?" Weird Wally was trying to push the lady's buttons and make her crazy and angry; his studio sidekicks were in the background, laughing with him as he made fun of the caller, and Anthony and I were laughing, too. "Did these interstellar cab drivers pop you out to our solar system's biggest tourist attraction?"

"No, Wally. Listen, Wally. I'm serious."

"I can tell you are."

"There's something going on in Teddle, Wally. You're the only one who can warn people, get it out. Nobody else will listen or talk about it."

"I don't want to talk about it either, lady."

"People are changing. Acting different. Those guards at the gates on the base? They don't even act human anymore, Wally. It's as if they're not even human anymore."

"How do I know you're human, lady? Right now that seems a stretch. Are you suffering from brain bubbles? Did you accidentally stick your head in the microwave along with your instant coffee this morning?"

The lady on the radio actually sounded sad now—in a way that almost scared me while I listened to her. "Why do you have to be this way, Wally? Why can't you just hear what I have to say?"

"I am hearing you, lady. Everybody with good sense in Teddle—meaning my loyal but stupid fans—is hearing you, but it's clear to me and everybody else that you are stone cold out of your mind and—"

Click. Ma switched off the radio as she came

back in the house from out back where she had been feeding the dog. "You guys know I don't like you listening to that crude individual."

"He's funny," I said as always.

"Not in the least," said Ma. Then: "How's the sneezing?"

I took a deep breath—all dry. "Nothing yet."

"That's good. How are you feeling? Dizzy? Tired?"

"Nope."

"Well, take it easy. Remember the doctor said there might be some effects."

We played some soccer in gym, which was cool because I love the game, but also because it shows I was feeling all right. A person cannot run around like a maniac, diving and kicking and maintaining his bearings, and not be feeling all right. I did so well I made a couple of friends. People are always much nicer to you when they figure out that you're not a complete loser.

Then after gym I had history, a quiet calm class with a quiet calm teacher called Mrs. Keller, which I point out to show that I wasn't a raving maniac after my soccer game. I was calm and normal and even knew that the Alamo was in Texas somewhere, and that's something history teachers in that state take very seriously.

And there was an interesting girl in that class with me, a straight-haired blond named Patty who was too serious for this world, and probably too serious for most any other world as well. I tried talking to her, only she wouldn't answer me, so I wrote her a note asking if she listened to Weird Wally in the morning, only she scribbled on the back of my note in red pen NO TALKING OR NOTES IN CLASS.

*Well, excuse me for living the wild life,* I thought, but I didn't attempt another note. Instead I stayed properly bored until history class ended, grabbed my stuff, and headed down the hall to my next destination—Room 104, my science class.

The overfriendly Ms. Patricia shared that class with me as well, and she followed me down the hall—keeping a safe distance—and waited for me to settle before she chose her seat, which she chose as far from me as she could while remaining in the same room. So I took the hint and began drawing on the back of my crisp new notebook with a felt marker I keep around for just such boring emergencies.

Bells were ringing now, and the teacher came in, and that, of course, is when it happened— that's what all this cynget, man in black, mysterious town creepiness has been leading to. My

**23**

mouth went dry, as if a dentist had slurped me with that suction thing they use, and my heart started pounding a *pitter-pat-pat* that must have sounded like a cranked up boom box. To this day I'm proud that I didn't scream. Anybody else would have.

I didn't scream. I lost my voice completely.

Because the teacher came in and with a green spade claw gripped the thick chalk and wrote MR. MANTIS on the blackboard, and he turned and he spoke, and what he said came out well enough except there was a roaring sound in my ears because the guy wasn't human. He had a shirt and a tie and very shiny shoes, but he also had green skin, antennae, and a claw mouth that quivered when he spoke, and his eyes were huge—they were a foot wide each, oval shaped, and they glistened like black leather.

My teacher was a bug.

# 4

# FAINTING WAS OUT OF THE QUESTION

Or at least it seemed like it at the time.

Breathing and feeling like a dog that had just accidentally caught the car it was chasing—out of breath and having no idea what to do now besides maybe chew on the tires—I looked around quick and held my pen tight, in case I needed it as a weapon, although I don't know what you could do with a pen when up against a bug monster man whose name is Mantis and who turns out to really be a mantis. Maybe write him a note begging not to be eaten. Except no notes were allowed in class. Remember. Patty wrote that to me in a note.

If this starts to sound hysterical and out of control, then it's an accurate report.

*Dream-check,* I thought. Is this a dream? One of those I'm-going-to-a-new-school-in-a-new-state nightmares?

No. Dreams felt one way, and life felt another, and this was feeling a lot like life in a bad-bugs-all-around way. So I looked about the class for somebody else who might be feeling as twisted and afraid as I was, only there was nobody. The closest was Ms. Patricia, except she didn't seem scared or terrified, she just looked bored—until she saw me staring at her. Then she looked annoyed.

My two new soccer buddies, Wayne and Mike, were in class, but they were muttering jokes to each other and laughing, and unless they had the All-Time Greatest Sense of Humor in the Face of Death Ever, they weren't on the same wavelength as me. Nobody was. These people were all in science class; their instructor was boring old Mr. Mantis. My teacher was a bug.

"This is seventh-grade general science," said Mr. Mantis, his antennae twisting together now and folding back over his huge green head. He smoothed them back with his claw in a way that looked almost stylish.

Stylish? What was I thinking about?

He was consulting a seating chart now, or at least I prayed it was a seating and not an eating chart. "Let's take the role," he said. "See if there's anybody who's not supposed to be here."

"Bingo!" I said, jumping up as if I'd just won something.

"Excuse me?" said the bug man.

"That's me," I said. "Wrong room, wrong place. Wrong guy. Not supposed to be here. Thanks. Sorry." I babbled my way forward, trying to get out of the class, working myself down the aisle to get clear of the desks so I could break for the door. Then I'd be all right; then I'd have a chance. Like I said, I'm fast.

"Uh, you're new," said Mr. Mantis, flipping a page with that hideous-looking paw-claw of his. "What's your name?"

"Name? No problem. I'm . . ."

Slam. That's when the second whammy came. I went completely blank: I could not remember my name.

I stood there, dulling it for a minute. Because I realized I not only couldn't remember my name, I couldn't remember my family—or if I even had a family. Or how old I was or where I came from. All I knew was the now, the immediate—Texas, classroom, unusually large and well-spoken insect.

The big bug monster guy said it again: "Uh, your name?"

Nothing from me.

The class started to laugh. Even under normal circumstances I would have seemed like a babbling idiot; the teacher was asking my name—that's all they could see—and I couldn't remember.

My panic mode seemed to last like an hour or so, but it was probably less than a minute, because then those brain-breakers started clicking back into place, and I ran through a checklist in my head.

Still alive? Yes.

Still able to think? Yes.

If this thing lunges at you with those claws, can you run? Absolutely.

"Come on, guy," said Wayne then—Wayne, my new soccer buddy. "Chill out."

"Yeah," agreed Mike.

Ms. Patricia was like most of the others: she just stared at me, waiting. Suddenly I knew how a fly on the wall really feels. He's not the one watching; he's the one terrified of being watched by everyone.

Mr. Mantis slurped again. "Are you all right, son?"

"No," I said, still trying to remember my name.

"I think I need to go to the nurse. I don't feel well."

Mr. Mantis nodded. Taking up a pen, he scribbled a note, and then this huge insect-guy handed me a pass to the nurse's office.

I ran.

Not remembering my name certainly didn't help my case at the nurse's office. Amnesia is not something the big woman in the stiff white uniform was used to dealing with, and I knew she thought I was kidding.

I wasn't. I tried everything to remember, even the old think back and hum to yourself from all those old parties: happy birthday to you, happy birthday to you, happy birthday dear—

And? Nothing.

Then I remembered my notebooks. My Teddle Junior High Class schedule. Of course! I looked inside and proudly announced to the nurse that I was Sullivan Ryan, didn't feel well, and needed to go home as soon as possible.

"Sullivan Ryan?" she asked, flipping through files. "You mean Ryan Sullivan?"

"Uh . . . yes, I do."

"What's wrong, Ryan?"

*MY TEACHER IS A BUG, THAT'S WHAT'S WRONG, MY TEACHER IS GREEN AND*

**29**

*LOOKS LIKE SOME HIDEOUS RADIOACTIVE MUTANT FROM A SCIENCE FICTION MOVIE AND WHAT KIND OF A PLACE IS TEXAS?!* That's what I thought, not what I said. What I said was the old reliable: "Uh . . . my stomach hurts."

About that the nurse seemed not very much concerned. "A lot of kids get stomachaches the first day of school," she said. She gave me an Alka-Selzer, made me lie down for ten minutes to settle my queasiness, then sent me back to class.

*Maybe this is me,* I thought, gathering my stuff and starting back toward my doom. *After all, I am on allergy medicine.* Who knew what that stuff could do to a person? Ryan Sullivan. Yeah, that was all coming back to me—my family, my jerk brother—it was all coming back like one of those instant photographs developing, but why had they gone away in the first place?

Science class was almost over. I walked very, very slowly, trying not to get back there before the bell.

Very, very slowly.

Creepy-crawl.

An insect's pace.

*Yeeech!* I just reached the classroom door when the bell rang. Yes! Kids were piling out and I just stood there, looking inside. Mr. Mantis turned, his big bug eyes looking out the door, seeing me.

Bugs have no eyelids; did you know that? Their eyes—those thousand little eyes making up two big ones—those eyes never close. They never blink. They never glance away. They just stare, seeing you.

More than seeing me. He's real, I thought. He's real, he's really a bug, this isn't a medicine thing—wouldn't everybody look like bugs if it was? He was real, and all of a sudden I knew that he knew I knew.

*He knows I know,* I thought.

He knew I knew.

In the second before I bolted down the hallway again, Mr. Mantis communicated with me, sent me a bug-to-kid message. In a smooth motion he raised his spade claw-paw to his mandibles like a person raising a finger to their lips, and he whispered, "Shhhhhhhhhhhh."

As in . . . don't tell anyone.

# 5

# In the Hallway of Doom

I thought seriously about running all the way back to California, but I didn't have my good sneakers on. Then, just when I figured nothing good could come of this bad craziness, something did. Or at least something interesting. As I was racing down the hallway, not even sure where I was going, Ms. Patricia ran to catch up and put a hand on my shoulder, grabbing and stopping me by some old brown lockers. "Hey," she said.

"Hey," I choked back.

Ms. Patricia came right to the point. "You can see them, can't you?"

That threw me. "What?"

"The bugs." Patty looked me straight in the eye, more defiant now. "The big, talking bugs. You're not laughing—you can see them, can't you?"

"Mr. Mantis," I said.

"Yeah," she answered, whispering now. "Keep your voice down. Yeah, he's one. Is he the only one you've seen?"

I wasn't used to being in conversations that did not compute. "Uh . . . my brain doesn't feel very well right now," I said. "I think it wants to go home and hide someplace. Under the bed or in a closet somewhere."

Ms. Patricia—Patty—shook her head. "I just wanted to tell you that you're not crazy. It's real. What you see in Mr. Mantis is real.

"It's a secret, though," she said. "You can't talk about it. If you start talking about it, they'll take you away."

"Take me away? What? To the funny farm?"

Patty shook her head. "No, to the base I think, and they do things out there to people that you wouldn't even want to think about."

"What?" That scared me. "My dad works at the base."

"Yeah? Well, everybody's dad works at the base. They work for the bugs. That's why they're still around."

"What's going on?"

"We can't talk about it. Not here, anyway."

"Not here? What?" I took a deep breath and

**33**

said, "Tell me what's going on. Write me a note or something."

"After school," she said, after just a moment's hesitation. "Wait for me at the flagpole after school; we'll walk home together. I guess it's okay to talk so long as nobody can hear us."

So Patty left me, and somehow I got through the rest of my day, then waited at the flagpole out front. Mr. Mantis walked out of school before Patty got there. I know he saw me, but he didn't chase after me. It took some guts on my part not to take off as soon as I saw him.

Patty showed up a few minutes later and we walked.

"I remember when I first saw," said Patty, telling the whole thing so calmly you might have thought she was talking about band practice. "It was the second week of summer, I was down at the pool, and I slipped on the deck; you know, tumbled right out of the hot into the cold water with all my clothes on. I hurt my arm doing it."

"Were you okay?"

"I didn't hit my head, just my arm, but nobody believed that. They thought I must have hit my head because when I came out I saw two big bugs—two guys from the base who were having their lunch and watching from a table. Only they were bugs, big yellow-and-black bugs."

**34**

"Yellow-and-black?"

"Bees. They were bees. They're not all like Mr. Mantis—Mantis, there's a joke. Some are bees, some are green bugs, some are ants. And wasps."

"Wasps?"

"Yeah," said Patty, quieter now. "They're the scariest."

I didn't ask why wasps were the scariest. I didn't want to know.

Patty finished her story. "I never thought I was crazy, but a lot of people would have. They sure would have. So after I stopped screaming I started watching. You know, to see if any more people looked like bugs to me. To see if everybody looked like a bug to me. Some did. Some still do. You see, you know."

I swallowed. "Are any of the other kids these bug things?"

"None that I've seen. It seems like only adults, the powerful people in town. The mayor. The police. Some of the teachers. And a lot of people from the base. I know this has something to do with the base."

"Have you told your mom and dad?"

"No way."

"Why not?"

Patty just looked at me.

"Aren't you scared?"

"No. Not really. Isn't that funny? It works that way, though. You'll see. You won't be scared. Well, you'll be scared, but it won't be like being really scared. It'll be the kind of scared that walking across the street in front of traffic is: so long as you're careful and look both ways you'll be all right."

Be all right. "How did you know I knew?"

Patty smirked—it wasn't really a smile. "The way you looked at him, the look in your eyes when Mr. Mantis gave you that hall pass. I thought you were going to run screaming from the room."

"I did run screaming from the room."

"You weren't screaming."

"I was screaming inside my head."

We walked a long way, talking about it and not much else. It wasn't as if we were getting to know each other. There wasn't anything else to talk about.

"How come everybody can't see that Mantis is a bug?" I asked.

"There are a lot of bugs in this town," she said again. "Go to the base now, now that you can see. All the guards are bugs—most of the people inside, too."

"But how come we can see but everybody else can't?"

"Pheromones."

"Fairy-a-what?"

"Pheromones. Chemicals the bugs put into the air to protect themselves. Normal bugs do it to attract mates or scare away bugs that might eat them, whatever. A lot of animals use pheromones like that, I guess, but they mostly work with what people call lower life forms."

*Lower life forms,* I thought. *Right.*

Patty must have known what I was thinking. "These superbugs use them to keep people from seeing what they really are. Unless something in you messes with the pheromones and keeps them from working. Do you believe in ESP?"

"Mind reading? No way."

"A lot of mind reading is just being able to see through the pheromones," said Patty. Then she said, "There's others of us, you know."

I didn't know what she meant, and I said so.

Patty explained: "There's a few of us who know about the bugs. Seven before, you make eight. It's sort of a club. We all know; we all realized on our own."

"I'm on allergy medicine," I said. "Maybe that let me see."

"Might have been at first. But once you know, it's easy to see. I didn't have to slip into the cold water again. It's like your eyes all of a sudden

**37**

know what to look for. You're immune to the pheromones; the bugs can't hide from you anymore. The only problem is you stop caring. You don't want to do something. I think that's the pheromones, too."

"Do something?" I didn't understand. "Do something about what?"

"Think about it," said Patty, leaving me then. "Be careful. And whatever you do, don't tell your mom or dad."

"Why not?"

"That's obvious. Think about that, too."

"Hey," I said.

"What?"

"Uh . . ." I felt stupid, but I had to know. "Do these bug guys eat people?"

Patty didn't answer. She just smiled, except it wasn't a very happy-looking smile.

And she left.

I did think about the Ma and Dad thing, and it wasn't too difficult to figure out they would start thinking I was the one with the problem. But I couldn't go home and sleep after all this without telling someone.

So that was when I sucked it up, sucked it in, took a really deep breath, and decided to do the scariest thing I could think of.

I decided to tell my big brother, Anthony.

# 6

# ANTHONY

My older brother wasn't as lucky as me, and instead of a new dramatic mission in life, he had come home from the first day of school with lots of homework.

He was settled at the kitchen table, surrounded by open books, and I said, "Hey, Anthony."

He didn't even look up. Instead he asked, "Do you know what the worst three words in the English language are?"

"Uh . . . 'You're under arrest?' "

" 'Show your work,' " he said, flipping over a long, scrawled page of algebra. To me it might as well have been a long poem written in Chinese. Anthony turned the book around to show me. "Progressive teacher," he said. "New math.

They've got all the answers in the back so you can check yourself, but you still get stuck doing the problems because the teacher wants you to 'show your work.' ''

Algebra, yeech, but that was ninth grade. I was going to be lucky to make it through seventh, but then I realized I'd probably be lucky to *live* through seventh grade, what with all that was happening.

"Hey," I said again. "Can I talk to you about something?"

"You always do," he said, looking at me. "You talk too much."

"I'm serious."

"So am I."

"Come on, listen."

"Okay." Anthony looked up, listening.

So I told him.

"Run that by me again," said Anthony about three minutes later, his lips pursed as if he might suddenly spit in three different colors.

I tried, telling it without exaggeration (or at least not so much). I told him about Mr. Mantis, everything that had happened that afternoon, as well as the stuff Patty told me.

"Oh, terrific," said my caring and loving brother. "Not only are you a nut, but you've managed to find the other school nut, too. Not bad for a first day."

"I'm serious," I said, settling down at the table across from him.

"You're seriously crazy, that's for sure."

Time-out here—obvious reason. Any story like mine is bound to wind up with a section like this. You know, the part where the person like me tries to convince the person (if you can call him a person) like my brother Anthony that some very weird thing is true, only who would believe it?

Well, this was a very weird thing, and Anthony didn't believe it. He thought I was trying to get him to go along as part of a practical joke, a gag, so I could make fun of him, suddenly scream, "Hooked! Fished you in!" and run around telling everyone what a gullible moron he was; we'd done it to each other before.

Anyway, everybody knows how this sort of scene goes, but the windup was Anthony finally nodding, closing his math book, and saying to me, "A bug."

"A real big bug."

"So?"

That startled me. "What do you mean, so?"

"So you've got a teacher who bugs you? Talk to Ma. What do you want me to do about it?"

"Not bugs me—he is a bug. A giant bug." Swallowing, I took a really deep breath and said, "I need you to come to school with me tomorrow morning."

"Hold it a second, bonehead," said Anthony, grimacing at me with that irritating I'm-the-smartest-one-I-know look. "How can I come to school with you if I have to go to school myself? Remember that high school thing I'm in? Hello?"

"You could ditch."

"No way. I did that once: remember who told on me to Ma and Dad?"

"I told you I was sorry. I won't do it again."

"You better believe it; I was grounded for a month. Did I ever get you back for that?"

"Anthony, man, I'm serious. I need you to come to school with me tomorrow."

He opened his math book again. "No way."

"Please."

"Forget about it."

"Come on, man. . . ."

"It's not happening."

"Anthony, I'm scared. . . ."

So he came with me.

The day started with Weird Wally as always; he was playing a phone prank on somebody who worked at the radio station.

Anthony and I weren't alone in the kitchen, of course. Dad was going in to work late that morning for some reason. We hardly ever saw him at breakfast, but today he was at the sink trying to concoct fresh orange juice without the seeds and the pulp.

"It's just about time for school, isn't it?" I asked. Hint, hint.

"There's a few minutes to spare," said Ma. "Isn't it nice that we all get to eat breakfast together for a change?"

"I'd settle for a decent glass of juice," said Dad.

"So what's up at the base?" asked Anthony, knowing Dad would never really say. "You guys making some nukes to zap the Russians?"

"The Russians are our friends now," Dad reminded him.

"Then who are our army and air force guys going to zap with your superweapons?"

Dad just smiled. "We're not building any superweapons."

"You've got to be building something."

"You know I can't talk about that."

"The army and air force don't build go-carts," said Anthony. "Anything you guys are working on out there—"

"Can only get us all in trouble if we discuss it," said Dad, joining us at the table.

**43**

"Okay, okay," said Anthony, whining just a lit-tle bit.

"How's school life?" asked Dad.

"Not bad for me," said Anthony. "Ryan's the one with the problem."

"Problem?" Dad frowned. "What is it? A bully?"

"Not exactly."

"What is it exactly?"

"Dad . . ."

Ma put a hand on his arm. "It's only the second day, honey. Give him a break. If he's got a prob-lem, he'll bring it to us. Won't you, Ryan?"

"Yeah." Except Patty and the others made it clear this was a secret sort of a problem. Except who could possibly keep this sort of thing a se-cret? I needed to tell somebody, even Anthony would do, and I was still more than ready to go, and kept looking at my brother and rolling my eyes so he'd get the hint. He was getting the hint; he was just choosing to torture me, but finally he got up and followed me out.

"Well, walking together," said Ma, impressed. "That's a pleasant change."

"Not so pleasant," said Anthony, but he fol-lowed me out of the house. "This better be good," he muttered as we walked.

"It's not good," I said. "If it was good, we wouldn't be doing this."

"You know what I mean."

"Yeah, whatever."

What the plan was supposed to be going into this great adventure, I didn't know; all I knew was I'd convinced my brother to come to school with me and be a witness, but I couldn't exactly take him into class with me, so we tramped around outside the building, trying to peek in the windows before school started, trying to figure out which room was Mr. Mantis's class. Nothing looked the same from outside.

Impatient as always, Anthony groaned at me. "Come on, bug hunter, you're the expert. Which window is it?"

"I'm not sure. Give me a minute."

"We're going to look like a couple of Peeping Toms."

"It's only school," I said. We looked around, and I finally found the window I thought peered into Room 104, the science class, and I pointed it out to Anthony. "I recognize it from the posters on the wall. Table of the elements and stuff."

"Fine," said Anthony. "Let's go see."

"We've got to sneak up, peek in. We can't just walk over and stare."

"Why not? Has this bug guy got some super death ray or something?"

He didn't believe me, but he soon would. "You'll see," I told him. "Just be careful," I warned.

"Yeah, right."

I followed my brother over to the window, and Anthony bounced about and peeked his head around to peer inside, still unconcerned about anything. Then he frowned, frowned some more, and opened his mouth.

Then Anthony screamed, "Oh my God!"

My blood went cold. . . .

# 7

# THE WIDE-AWAKE CLUB

"What?" I jumped, jerked, and if Anthony hadn't grabbed me, I would have bolted.

"You are such an idiot," he laughed, pulling away.

"What? Wasn't he in there?"

"Sure, there's a teacher in there. Short little old guy. But he didn't look like no bug."

I peeked around myself. *Yeeech*. Mr. Mantis, all right, green and fluttering around his desk and the blackboard. So why couldn't Anthony see him?

I thought quickly, then remembered: "The pheromones."

"What?"

"We can't see him now."

"No? Why can't we?"

"I mean you can't." I was trying to think of a reasonable way to explain this all. Where was Patty when I needed her?

Anthony wasn't ready to wait around. "Ryan, I've got stuff to do. I've got more homework than I've ever seen before in my life. I need to get to school."

"You mean leave me?"

"Yes, dimwit, I mean leave you here at this dangerous junior high school full of enraged insects." He started to walk off.

"Anthony, wait, listen." I grabbed him by the arm, rambling on. "All I mean is you can't see, but I want you to see, only you'll probably have to do something special to see."

"Like what? Wear those X-ray glasses from the back of the comic book ads? Well, sorry, I don't have any."

Thinking quickly, I said, "It takes something to shake up your brain and help you see."

"Forget it, then," he said. "No way am I letting you shake my brain."

"Not really shake . . . I mean . . ."

I shut up for a second; this was sounding worse all the time. "Well, I'm on the allergy medicine."

"So what do you want me to do? Go get a shot like you did? Is that what you're trying to con me into?"

"No, no," I said. "Patty fell into a swimming pool with her clothes on. That did it for her."

"Fell into a pool with her clothes on." Anthony nodded but didn't say anything at first, not until he'd thought for a few seconds. Then his frown lifted and he smiled, nodding at me. "I get you now. That's what all this is about—you're trying to trick me into doing something really stupid like you probably did on your first day. Well, if you think I'm jumping into a pool with my clothes on, or anything else stupid, forget about it."

"Anthony, really . . ."

"Forget it. I am out of here," he said, leaving me. "Good luck. Maybe for your birthday I'll buy you a can of Raid! Hah!"

Thus began my second day of school.

Ms. Patricia, the anti-note person, passed me a note in history class. All it said was "Flag-pole—3:15."

I followed her to my bug class.

Which was interesting, because Mr. Mantis kept giving me these knowing looks, letting me know he knew what I was seeing. Or at least that's what I thought he was doing.

Now, another obvious question needs to be answered here, which is this: if you knew your teacher was a bug, why would you ever go near the class again?

There was no reason not to go. Bug or not, he hadn't attacked me or anybody else so far as I knew. Not yet, anyway, and Patty said it wasn't going to happen. What my teacher was interested me but the more I thought about it, the less actual fear I felt.

So it sounds stupid, but here it is: I was curious.

What was going to happen next?

I wondered the whats of a lot of things.

*What must it be like being a bug teacher in a world full of humans?* I wondered. It had to be like forever wondering if somebody was staring at you because you'd spilled mustard on your shirt or because one of your antennae was showing.

Did bugs eat mustard?

What did Mr. Mantis eat?

I correct myself: there were a few scary questions that were still nagging at me.

After all, you don't need to hate dogs to want to avoid the ones who bite.

At the flagpole after school, Patty said, "Some friends of mine want to talk to you."

I looked around. "Where are they?"

**50**

"Come and see."

So I wound up at a meeting in the basement of Quentin Meyer's house. He was a year older than all of us. Quint had a name for this growing group of his—the Wide-Awake Club. I thought that sounded a lot like some Saturday morning kids show and Patty agreed with me, but Quint insisted, and most of the others didn't care what we called ourselves.

Terri Van Gelder was a red-haired girl from the church school, which meant we didn't see her during the day, but she said the bugs were there as well and nobody else seemed to notice them. "I've got two teachers who look like Mr. Mantis, and the janitor looks like something I've never seen before. Gray."

"Old, you mean?"

"And green."

"Oh."

Everybody at the meeting explained how they came to realize what was going on. Terri was first. "It was milk that started me," she said. "It was a really hot day and I wanted something to drink, and everybody was drinking Kool-Aid but I wanted chocolate milk and I poured a glass and swigged it—only the milk was spoiled."

"Yuck," said Amy Polson.

"It was clumpy and lumpy and sour, and I spit

**51**

the milk into the sink and was gagging and trying to run some water, and that's when I looked out the window and saw the mailman was a bug."

"What did you do?"

"I fainted. They thought it was the milk."

Most of the stories were like that; some sudden jolt to the system. With Mike Ploen it actually was—he accidentally stuck his finger in a light socket while trying to plug in a stereo. "Got 110 volts and a good view of my insect neighbor mowing his lawn," he said. "I thought I was dead."

"I want to know what we're going to do about it," I asked.

Most of them didn't seem to understand my question. Especially Terri, who looked like she'd been punched, but Patty was the one who said, "Do about it? What's there to do about it?"

"It's like the spider and the fly," Quint explained. He sounded embarrassed. "The bugs are doing something to our minds so we don't care so much. When the spider comes for the fly, at first he struggles, but then . . . well . . . the fly doesn't care so much anymore."

I pictured a housefly struggling in a spider web—terrified, doomed, relaxing for what was coming. Then I pictured myself as the fly and didn't feel so much like relaxing.

"No way," I said. "I sure don't feel that way."

**52**

"You will."

I shook my head but didn't argue. "So how did you guys get together?"

"Over a while, not all at first," explained Patty.

"What about Quint?" I asked, motioning over to him.

"Oh, that was funny," said Patty. "Quint came right up to me in the park and asked me if I knew a good exterminator."

I laughed, but I said, "I'm feeling just a little bit paranoid. I told my brother," I said.

That surprised them, but Patty was the one who cared the most. "That wasn't smart," she said.

"I'll admit that; he's pretty crude."

"You shouldn't talk to anyone besides us."

"Why not?"

"If you were hiding in the dark, you wouldn't keep switching on a flashlight, would you?"

"So you all know what's going on," I said again. "What are you guys going to do about it?"

"What are you talking about?" asked Victor Ramos. "There's nothing to do."

"Nothing to do yet," said Quint.

"Yeah?"

"What I mean is this," said Quint. "We stay low, keep quiet, and watch what happens."

"Right up until the bugs take us away like the others."

Finally. They were starting to fight the argument I'd started, but now something scary had come out again. Getting information from these so-called wide-awake people was like pulling teeth. "Others? What others?"

"There's more of them out there than just a few big green bugs who control a few minds, who make people see things that aren't there."

"We don't want anything to happen," said Quint.

"We don't want to get taken away," said Terri.

"What are you talking about?"

Vic explained. "You know all those empty houses? Everybody's supposed to think people just moved away because of cutbacks at the base. But nobody's moving away. Nobody ever moves away."

"So what happens to them?"

"The wasps, probably."

"Don't talk about the wasps," said Patty.

"At first there were only a few wasps—a lot of bugs, but only a few wasps. Now there's a lot more."

"Don't talk about the wasps," said Patty again. This put a hush over everything; I could feel the chill myself.

"Why not?" I asked.

"It's a rule," Quint reminded everyone.

"Forget the rule," I said. "Let's change the rule. What about the wasps?"

"Hey—" Quint was suddenly so angry he shut himself up. He was pushing me back, making me leave the basement. "Nobody knows anything for real, and you're just going to scare everybody."

That made no sense at all. "If everybody knows but me, how am I going to scare anyone?"

But I could see what he was talking about, because right away Terri started to cry and gathered her stuff together. "Club meeting is over," said Quint, and it sure was. Everybody was leaving now.

Talk about avoiding a subject. . . .

"Vic, man," I said, following him up the stairs. "Come on, what's this wasp thing?"

He wouldn't answer, just shook his head. "Bug teachers are no big deal. Can't be prejudiced; not even all the bugs are bad. The wasps are the scary ones."

"How do you know this?"

Patty was the one who answered, coming up the stairs behind me and following me outside and across Quint's yard, heading down the street. This was about the same time I noticed that Quint's street was one of the empty-looking ones, with more than a few houses standing like tombs with the drapes closed. Patty whispered, saying, "Even quiet voices talk sometimes." She looked around a minute. "It's hard not to hear things."

"So are you going to tell me this wasp story, or am I supposed to guess it's ten times worse than it is?"

"You could never guess that high," she said.

# 8

# THE MAN IN BLACK

It was at some point after this that the man in black snuck into town.

None of what was happening to me and the Wide-Awake Club would have exactly startled the man in black; of course, he was the sort of guy not easily startled. He believed in too many things, being aware, as he was, that too many things were real—things that should never have been real, such as man-eating plants, storms where it rained frogs, and people who spontaneously burst into flame.

The man in black read a lot—mostly tabloids—and he rarely watched TV unless there was a news show covering something that fell into his area of interest. And he contemplated all of it, which is a fancy way of saying he thought it all over again and again, trying to make sense of things that mostly made no sense. Then he wrote reports on what he had learned and sent them on to higher authorities he wasn't even sure existed.

He was strong, sure, confident. He was the man in black.

And right now, he was also lost.

"Excuse me," he said to the man at the Texaco station on the outskirts of town, "but I seem to have misplaced the interstate highway. What town is this?"

"Teddle," said the attendant, stepping closer to the open driver-side window to admire the new black sedan. The gas station attendant had a horrible backache, a gnawing, slow sort of pain between his shoulder blades that was distracting him that afternoon, but he was a good, polite guy and always curious. "What kind of a car is this?"

"This? Oh, just a G.O.V."

"G.O.V?"

"Government-Owned Vehicle."

"Government man? You looking for the base?"

"Base?"

"Teddle Base."

"Teddle? Hmmm, Teddle, Teddle, Teddle ..." the man in black murmured as he appeared to sort through a pile of maps. His face did not in the least betray the shock he felt because he knew there shouldn't be a Teddle Base. He didn't need a map—his memory was photographic. That was one of the reasons he was chosen to be the man in black.

The man in black knew the names and locations of every army, navy, air force, and marine base in the country. He also knew the names and locations of the fourteen ultra-top-secret bases in the country that even the president wasn't supposed to know about.

There used to be a Teddle Base—sure, he remembered that. It was an old army training base during World War II, long since closed. Certainly there was nothing operating there now.

Still, the name rang a bell in his head and the man in black believed in coincidences; happenstance was sometimes the way the universe reorganized itself. The maps were one thing, but what he was really looking for was to be found in an old, yellowing issue of the *International Quest-News,* a rag he'd discovered in a Seattle Laundromat one morning—April Fools' Day, in fact.

Ah, yes . . . indeed. A stack of cattle mutilation stories and UFO sightings and hysterical tales of secret desert bases that made Nevada's Area 51 seem like Disneyland.

The man in black knew a little bit about the

truth behind cyngets, UFOs, flying saucers, whatever you wanted to call them. He knew a lot of them could travel millions of light-years to earth but would then crash for no logical reason, and he knew people often claimed to have been taken for a ride, usually people with questionable IQs, and he knew this had gone on for years without any serious incident.

Until recently, of course, when the flying saucers changed, seeming to go from being controlled by strange, childlike aliens to being controlled by strange, insectlike bugs. There was a new sheriff in town in the skies over America, and it may or may not have been a problem, but the man in black had once wondered if Teddle, Texas, might have something to do with the changes going on.

Now he was here, but he'd never quite realized where here was. Teddle, Texas.

Best to put the old thinking cap on. . . .

I wasn't aware of any of this yet, though. I, Ryan Sullivan, had my own insect problems.

A couple of days after the Wide-Awake Club meeting and the mysterious wasp discussion I did something I'd never done before in my life: I called Weird Wally's radio show. I figured I was safe since Ma wouldn't let us listen to it if she was around, so she and Anthony weren't about to hear me.

I pulled the living-room extension phone into the closet and shut the door; it took about six tries to get through. Some guy answered the phone for Weird Wally, and I didn't beat about the bush: I told him why I was calling. He put me right through.

"Go ahead, you're on the air," said Weird Wally. His voice sounded as if it were echoing in a tunnel. I could hear snickering in the background.

I swallowed. "Wally, there's something you should know."

"I know most everything, but try me."

"Bugs."

"Excuse me?"

Whispering, I said, "My teacher is a bug."

"A lot of teachers are bums."

"Not bum, bug. He's a giant insect."

"Uh-huh . . ." There was a click and at first I thought he'd hung up on me, because I heard a commercial playing on the radio, but Weird Wally's voice was back in my ear, only not in an echo now. "Who is this?"

Standing there in the dark closet, I closed my eyes and it only got darker. "I . . . I can't say."

"You'd better say." Weird Wally sounded even more annoyed than usual.

"No."

"Fine. Well, listen, kid. Are you a smart kid?"

"Yeah. I mean, I think so. Sort of smart."

"Sort of smart. Right. Well, you better stop talking about this bug teacher of yours if you know what's good for you."

That was scary. "What's good for me?"

Weird Wally exploded: "I'LL TELL YOU WHAT'S GOOD FOR YOU KID! BECAUSE I'M A BUG MYSELF, YOU STUPID TWERP, AND I DIDN'T COME ALL THIS WAY TO HAVE IT ALL BLOWN BY SOME PUNK KID WHO THINKS HE'S A HERO! AND I'M TRACING THIS CALL!"

Slam! I jumped away from the phone, my heart practically exploding.

While I was at school, of course, it occurred to me that I probably wasn't the first one to try and alert Weird Wally to what was happening in town, and being the obnoxious person he was, that was more than likely how he dealt with people he thought were freaks.

Either that or he was a bug.

As always, Mr. Mantis's science class was the highlight of my day. My grades everywhere else were going into the tank because my concentration had never been good and was now nonexistent. Funny. Just the second week of school and my future was being muddled up by a six-foot-tall insect.

Future?

Mr. Mantis was starting the year with what he called environmental science: "Understanding the effect your actions have on the world as a whole. Remember the old story—if a butterfly flaps his wings in China, the weather changes in Texas."

"Tell him to get flapping, then," said Wayne.

That got a laugh, but not from me. To me, it was just one bug telling me another bug controlled not only my destiny but my weather. Terrific.

After school was interesting. No flagpole huddles or secret basement meetings, but when I got home, there, on the kitchen table, was a note from Anthony. It said:

*Ryan—*
   *DON'T TALK TO ANYONE. You were right. I've seen them—I've seen the bug guys, and we've got to do something.*

*I don't know what. But I know something
bad is happening.*

*I wonder if Dad knows? This probably has
something to do with the base!*

The note was signed by Anthony.

*Well,* I thought with such relief that it surprised me, *it's about time.* But why was he leaving a note? Why not just talk to me?

The house was awfully quiet.

"Ma?" I yelled. "Anthony? Hello?"

No answer. I walked through the house, heading upstairs. Finally, I thought. Maybe we could
be a team on this. Anthony wasn't so bad when
he wasn't acting like a louse. And he was really
great on a bike. That was the sort of thing that
could come in handy.

I went across the hall to his room and pushed
open the door. "Anthony? Yo, Anthony, I—"

Anthony wasn't there.

Instead, a giant black ant lunged for me,
screeching, "Die, human, die! Arrrrrrr-
gggggghhhhhh!"

# 9

## ASSEMBLY

To say I screamed would be an exaggeration; screaming requires more output than I possibly could have managed. What I did was gasp, slip, fall, and land on my rear in the hall, close my eyes, and wait for the end.

The end was, of course, laughter.

Anthony—Anthony laughing.

This time, though, I bolted up, really angry. "You jerk!"

Muffled beneath a rubber ant-head mask, Anthony was gasping himself, gasping in laughter. "What a gulli-bull," he was saying. "What a nitwit."

"Nitwit? You—you—"

"Me, me, me," said Anthony, laughing. He pulled off the ant-head mask, sucked for some fresh air, and kept laughing, saying, "You should have seen the look on your face—"

Anthony wiped the sweat from his brow. "I thought you were going to choke and die. It was so cool!"

"Thanks a lot."

"It was great. I spent thirty dollars on this mask. I had to borrow against my allowance, but I'll use it at Halloween, I guess. It was definitely worth it. Oh, yeah, this was worth it. You stupid dweeb. . . ."

For a while I considered booby-trapping my bedroom to keep the bugs and moron brothers out, but I couldn't convince myself that it was necessary.

I managed to make myself so nervous I prowled around the kitchen for a while, as if I might find answers there. Ma asked what I was doing, but I mumbled something about just looking for a brown paper sack.

"So what do you need a brown paper sack for?"

"Uh . . ." I reached for the first answer I could come up with. "I've got to make something for school."

"What's that?"

"It's sort of a secret," I said, noticing then that

Ma was suddenly frowning, as if she was in pain. "What's wrong?"

Her smile came right back. "Nothing, honey, just a little backache. It'll go away."

"Right." There weren't any brown paper bags, but there was a can of insecticide in the cupboard, down with the laundry detergent and a can of paint, but that probably wouldn't have had any effect on these guys. I read an article once in school about how insecticide was ruining the environment, and one of the things it said was bugs were becoming immune to all but the deadliest pesticides anyway. Pretty soon they'd be immune to those as well, it said, and we would be living with a generation of superbugs.

Say hello to pretty soon, I thought.

That next morning when I grabbed my stuff and headed out I got another unscary surprise: Ms. Patricia was standing at the end of the walkway, waiting for me. "I wanted to talk to you," she said.

"Okay," I said. She fell into step.

Patty came right to the point. "You've got to stop talking to people."

"What?"

"Ryan, I heard your brother bought an ant mask."

"Yeah, he's a jerk."

"He told everybody he knows that his little brother thinks he can see giant bugs running around town."

"Where did you hear that?"

"I hear things. It's dangerous. So dangerous."

"You know what I'm starting to think? I think this is all a really different, really strange dream—"

"Ryan—"

"Hear me out," I said, looking her in the eye and laying it all out. Yeah, it even made sense to me if I said it out loud. "I used to have nightmares before, when I was a little kid, and I figured out a way to fight them, and that was to fight them."

"Ryan, this isn't a dream."

"Hey, it's either a dream or life is really out of whack. Either way, I know I need to fight for my life."

"Your life isn't in danger."

"I don't know about that. I've got a funny feeling it is. What about this wasp thing?"

"We don't know anything about the wasps."

I stopped and stared at Patty a minute. "You're funny, you know that? You're the first one to clue me in that I'm not crazy, that this is all real, and

**68**

you're always the one trying to keep me from doing anything about it."

"You're going to get us all in big, big trouble," said Patty very seriously. Ms. Patricia decided to leave me then, but I called after her, almost cackling, "Maybe I need to fight for your life, too."

I laughed again. Sheesh, I was standing there outside the school laughing by myself. Maybe I did have a problem.

Mr. Mantis was his usual green self, but he didn't look at me much. It was as if we had a silent communication. Oh yeah, I thought sarcastically. Me and the bug guy, we got this understanding. He don't assign homework, I don't plug a bug zapper in the teacher's lounge.

Despite being a bug, he was still trying to teach science, and this amused me because the science he was teaching didn't exactly seem to fit into the seventh grade. "Today," he said, "let's talk about the future of the world."

"Is this science or science fiction?" someone asked.

"Well, let's think about it," said my teacher the bug. His antennae twitched, but I'd found if I stared and squinted enough I could almost make out what he was pretending to be—what the other kids were seeing—a little old man in a tweed suit. Probably that was dangerous on my part. I figured it was possible to concentrate too hard and start believing in him myself.

Probably that would have been for the best. But it wasn't happening.

"Extinction," said Mr. Mantis.

"What's that?" asked one of the dumber kids.

I already knew.

"Extinction is when all the animals of one species die, and there are no more left to carry on. Like the dinosaurs," Mr. Mantis continued.

"Oh. Wow."

"Does anyone know how many species of life on earth go extinct every year? Hundreds. Humans are devastating their world. This is the time of most extinctions since the time of the dinosaurs, when a comet the size of Manhattan hit the planet."

"Did everything die back then?" asked one of the girls in class.

"No." It was Patty who answered, not Mr. Mantis. "The insects survived."

"Yes," agreed my teacher the bug. "And the smaller mammals."

I looked over at Patty. Her eyes seemed cold; maybe I was getting to her, or maybe it was Mr. Mantis. Either way, he went on and on about extinctions and how we were ruining the planet and how somebody ought to do something about it because "variety of species is essential to the survival of all species," but I was so preoccupied with what he was that I never made any connection with what he was saying. Certainly there was no message in it for me.

Except there was.

There was a school assembly set for that afternoon, and the principal, Mr. Nader, was introduced, and I scrunched lower into my seat because Mr. Nader was a bug, too, and his sudden appearance and speech were all the perspective I needed.

He was a wasp.

Time-out for a quick description here: a superwasp acting out the role of a junior high school principal is not exactly your run-of-the-mill wasp, the sort Ma finds nesting in the attic and calls for Dad to come and kill.

Mr. Mantis, he was a bug—green, big eyes, all that—and over the last two weeks he had begun to looking interesting to my eyes, but more or less docile, like a big hairy dog who never bites.

Nader the wasp was hideous.

Thin, thinner than any human could be and live, this wasp-creature was dressed not in human clothes, which would have fallen right off him, but in armor; a metallic-looking outfit right out of an old Roman Empire movie.

He had wings, too, but I didn't catch that at first because they were flapping so fast as to be almost invisible. All I heard was the buzz noise echoing through the auditorium.

Growing louder, because he wasn't the only one making the buzz. I took a desperate look around and saw others at various corners of the hall, several wasps, all focused on Nader at the microphone. All buzzing.

So ... Mr. Nader-Wasp stepped up to speak—or buzz, I guess—and his hands-claws moved quickly, too quickly, and his eyes were evil.

Nader would have killed me on sight: this much I knew.

"Today," he said through the buzz, "today we educate you on the New Order of things. The world as it shall be. Your world, our world. Our world, your obedience.

"Obey and live," said the wasp. "Disobey and die."

Die.

That's what I heard, anyway, through the buzz. What the other kids were hearing I had no idea, but it obviously wasn't the same thing. Unless, I thought, unless that was the point of this assembly, this buzz: to make sure everyone heard the message, but only at the back of their ears, the back of their minds.

That was so they could remember the scary message, know it, but never remember actually having heard it.

If I closed my eyes, he could be an ordinary principal, speaking of discipline and the upcoming year and all that nonsense. But maybe not. There was too much else to his sound than his voice, a high-pitched humming that echoed around the assembly and got into my ears and ate into my brain. It was like what a saber-toothed tiger growl must have been to a caveman. It grabbed you and chilled you and could not be ignored.

*So,* I thought, *there you are.*

Rather calmly because a lot of the teachers down there were bugs, just like Mr. Mantis. Not all of them, but a lot of them. And there were other bugs in the auditorium, huddled in the back, just sort of watching over everyone.

Like guards.

Bees, I noticed. Most of those seemed to be bees, with a few wasps thrown in, as if the bees were soldiers and the wasps officers.

And, so, was this the deal? Was this what

Patty had warned me about? The fact that bees and wasps were soldiers, the really bad guys?

I started to feel I was suffocating in there.

I don't do well at school assemblies in normal places, but there in bug city it was absolutely giving me the willies, so I decided, very rationally I thought, to get out of there. "I'm leaving," I said.

"What?" said Patty.

"Watch me," I said, standing up and shuffling down the row. Everybody assumed I had to go to the bathroom, so they didn't really make any trouble for me.

The big auditorium door slammed and echoed down the empty hallway. Look around, I thought; forget this nonsense. This is the last time I'm coming to this school until they go through it with a bunch of exterminators armed with machine guns.

That was when I ran into him, the big guy walking the hallway. I squinted, trying to figure out who he was really supposed to be—a janitor, teacher, whatever—but squinting didn't help because all he looked like was what he was: a six-foot-tall, plump yellow jacket.

I swear, I still heard—felt—that buzzing coming from somewhere.

I got a little fresh as I walked by Mr. Buzz, or

whatever his name was. I said, "You know, one time when I was nine my brother and I caught a bunch of honey bees in a jar. Those bees thought they were so tough."

That's when he stung me.

# =10=

# THE STING

I woke up in the nurse's office, still tingling all over. As always the room reeked of alcohol and the nurse's lavender perfume. I sat straight up on the cot and shouted: "Ow!"

Being stung by a bee or a hornet is a lot like getting zapped by electricity while somebody jabs a thick needle into you. Or so I always thought. I woke up trembling, as if I'd been buried alive in a thousand tons of dirt and suddenly been pulled free, gasping for air.

"You're better now," said the nurse.

She was seated behind me, so I turned and said, "Better? I should be dead—I was stung by a giant bee."

The nurse frowned, not exactly Mrs. Compassion. "You slipped on some spilled soda and hit your head."

"Hit my head?" What was this? Who was she trying to kid? She was a human, so far as I could tell. "I was stung. There must be a mark."

I looked at my arm. No mark.

"What did you guys do?" I asked.

"We brought you down here when you slipped and fell during the assembly."

"No, I mean about my arm." I pushed at it with a finger. It was tender, all right, but there was no big grotesque sting mark. "Unless," I said out loud, "unless it's there and I can't see it because of some pheromone thing to make me think I didn't get stung."

"Excuse me?" said the nurse. She was blinking fifty times a minute, it seemed.

"How are you feeling?" asked the nurse. "Can you remember your name this time?"

"Very funny," I said. I replayed the stinging incident in my head—there was no amnesia this time. A normal bee carries his stinger on the rear of his abdomen, but these superbees didn't bother with that. Don't read too much into it, though. Humans don't have tails anymore, either. But we carry guns and the superbees carried stingers on the end of long, thin sticks that looked like spears

**77**

with daggers and small rubber venom sacks attached to the end.

The sack was the scary thing, and the last thing I'd seen before going into shock, if shock was what you could call what happened to me. It was like a knife with a pouch attached, and when you got stuck with the knife the stuff that was in the pouch squirted into you. Except when a regular bee stung you, the very act was suicide; their stinger ripped their guts out when the bee tried to fly away. Superbees had that beat. Their portable stinger sacks looked refillable.

Wonderful.

Only worker bees sting; I'd read that. And bee stings are poison, I remembered from my recent bug research. More people die from bee stings every year than from spider or snake bites.

Maybe that was it. Maybe I was going to die.

That terrified me for all of ten seconds, until I realized that if you're going to kill someone with a superbee stinger, you don't truck them down to the nurse's office afterward. I wasn't supposed to be stung, and this was to fix it.

Which absolutely, positively proved to me that the nurse—human or not—was in on this thing, whatever the thing might be.

"Ryan . . ."

"You're in on all this, aren't you?" I asked, side-stepping around the room, wary and nervous. "This has got to happen every year, every couple of months." As soon as I said it out loud it made sense to me. "A kid realizes what's really going on in this town, gets all sick about it. He comes down to see you and gets sent off with an aspirin and some story about slipping on spilt soda or being nervous about school."

"I'm sure I don't know what you're talking about, Ryan." Her eyes were ice.

Mr. Mantis came in then and spoke quietly with the nurse. Then she left me alone with him. Oops.

A tall, green, utterly distinguished insect figure. He made a noise that in a human would have been a grunt; in an insect it sounded like air being sucked in through a tunnel and hissed right back out an opening in the back of the head.

Pheromones don't bother me at all, I thought to myself. For one reason or another, I'm the most perceptive person on the planet.

Wonderful.

Mr. Mantis spoke: "Would you like a ride home?"

"What? No."

"The buses have gone. You've missed your friends. I could—"

"No." I barked it out, then regretted it. What if he realized that I was on to him?

Of course, how could he not know I was on to him? If he didn't, what did all that "shhhhhhhhh" nonsense mean? I was too loud in the hallways? Not likely.

"Don't let your perceptions fool you," said Dr. Mantis. "Talk to your friends," he advised in a grandfatherly way. Right, my grandfather the praying mantis. Still, he said, "Listen to your friends. They can help you."

At first I didn't know what he meant, and then I did, sort of, because for a second he wasn't that bug monster. For a flickering second he was just a graying old school teacher. It was like the TV set in my head couldn't get the channels tuned in clearly, but I squinted and remembered who— what—I was looking at.

And Mr. Mantis was still a bug.

A bug offering me a ride home. Sheesh, how could he possibly get his big bug head into a car? Unless maybe he had some special bug car, and it only looked like a normal car to everyone because that's what they expected to see. Maybe if I looked at his car now I'd see something weird— some insect tank car or something.

This was all so crazy it made you, well, crazy.

Maybe he even realized that. Because he

**80**

twitched a little, stared at me with a thousand eyes, and then left the nurse's office.

Walking home, I came across Terri Van Gelder, and she was sitting on her front porch, crying, so I couldn't just walk by. Her mom and dad had one of the bigger houses in town, in the older, southern plantation style with white columns on the front porch, although not as large as they might have been in Georgia or Mississippi. This was southern Texas, and her family, after all, sent her to church school.

"Hey," I said, approaching her. "What's going on?"

At first she didn't say anything. Just kept crying, looking me in the eye now and then but not saying anything. "Come on," I said. "Can I help?"

"The lump," she finally whispered.

"The what?"

"The lump. My mom and dad both have the lump."

"What lump? What are you talking about?"

I didn't think she was going to answer, but then Terri seemed to find some courage somewhere inside herself and she said, "All the empty houses, all the people who supposedly moved away with their kids. Well, we know different. They were lumped."

"Lumped?" That sounded funny, except I had

**81**

a sick feeling in my stomach that it wasn't funny. "What does lumped mean? Come on, I'm new around here. Nobody tells me anything."

"I can't," she said, shaking her head. "Go read about it, why don't you?"

"Read about it? Where am I supposed to read about it? That doesn't make any sense."

"Yeah, it does. It's the wasps, I know. We know. Only we thought it would never happen to us, not to our parents. Oh, no," Terri laughed, but it was a mean laugh, through her tears, and obviously it still wasn't funny. "We were all supposed to keep quiet, play along, and it would never happen to our parents."

"What is it?"

"Look it up, it's in the encyclopedia, sheesh. It's no secret, except to us. Now Patty and Quint will tell everybody I moved away with my parents and they're still safe. . . ."

Terri was really crying then, really upset, but I didn't know what to do. "Go away," she finally said. "Just go away; there's nothing you can do."

Nothing, I thought, except take her advice and look it up. Could it be that simple? Were all the answers at home in the encyclopedia all along?

I didn't know what to think, though. I'd been stung and survived—what was the big deal?

What was this lump thing? Where did the people from the empty houses go? Why was Terri crying?

On my way home I got part of the answer. I was getting ready to cross Main Street when I saw a convoy of three army trucks headed through town, out from the base, and at first I thought nothing of it, except the back flap of one of the trucks blew open and before the guys could pull it closed I saw them inside, dozens of them, bright yellow and black they were, but eyes as dead as open space.

Bees. The trucks were full of bees wearing strange uniforms, leaving the base and heading out to the world.

And across the street from me, watching this bug army deploy, was this weird short dude in a thin dark tie, jacket, shoes, and a hat.

The man in black.

# II

# KAFKA WHO?

When I saw the bee thing, considered along with Principal Nader-Wasps' buzz speech at the school assembly, I realized something that nobody in the so-called Wide-Awake Club had figured out yet: this was no weird accident or a couple of lost creatures from another planet. This was a full-scale invasion coming from somewhere!

One thing I couldn't figure out, though, was that man in black I'd seen across the street. Something about the guy struck me as both scary and reassuring, as if a monster were here to strike dead the bugs, and he might kill me in the process, but so be it.

Except the man in black didn't really seem a monster. He seemed like ... well ... a magician.

No, better yet: a spy.

**84**

That's what he was; I knew right away. He was a spy.

But a spy for whom? For what?

What was he supposed to be?

All the kidding around was over now, all fears of Anthony's mocking, Patty's warnings, and whatever else. The terrified look on Terri's face was something I couldn't get out of my head.

Bad things were happening.

There had to be a way to get past this pheromone thing, and it was time to tell Ma and Dad everything I knew.

Anthony was in the living room. "Hey, bug-a-boo," he said.

"Don't start with me." I glared. There was serious business ahead.

"I just wanted to tell you that I accidentally stepped on some of your buddies outside. Ants, I think they were. Some sort of bugs, anyway."

*He sure didn't step on any of those bugs from the assembly,* I thought, walking. When I came into the kitchen, Dad was rinsing potatoes in the sink and Ma was on the phone, saying something like, "Well, that's good to know about him."

Good to know about whom?

"Yes," she said. "Yes, I'm sure."

I went over to my father. "Dad, can we talk?"

"Always can," he said.

"This is weird stuff," I warned him. "But I need you guys to believe me."

"Us guys? Did you want to wait until your mother gets off the phone?"

I shook my head. "It can't wait. We can tell her, but first you've got to listen and believe me."

"Okay, shoot."

I took a deep breath, but barely got out Mr. Mantis's name before Ma was hanging up the phone and joining the conversation. "Mr. Mantis?" she said.

"Yeah," I breathed, trying to choke it all out.

"Well, what a coincidence. That was him just now on the phone."

Time-out for just a quick second of brainlock. Then: "Say what?"

Ma shrugged. "He called to tell me about how you slipped at school but how you were all right. We talked about some other things. He thinks you're upset about the move."

"Move?" I had no idea what she was talking about.

"The move from California to Texas."

I made that point again: "I am not upset about the move."

"Well, he thinks you must miss old friends."

"Of course I miss old friends—that's not the point."

"So what is the point?" wondered Dad.

I gave that a moment's thought, trying to think of the best way to plunge into all this. "Have you noticed that there are no dogs in town?"

"So what are you now? The dogcatcher?" Anthony was on a roll.

"No. Just passing along a scary piece of information I learned from the Wide-Awake Club."

"The who?" asked Ma.

"What's so scary about it?" wondered Dad.

"Yeah, I hadn't even noticed," said Ma. Dad nodded as if he thought it was interesting as well, but no big deal. "No late-night barking to keep a person awake."

"Not just dogs. Cats. Birds. Gerbils, turtles, hamsters. Nothing."

"Well, I don't know," said Dad, after thinking a moment. "Maybe people in this part of the country aren't much into pets."

"Not even one?"

"What are you trying to say, Ryan?"

"I'm trying to say that people don't keep pets here because no pet in his right mind would live here."

He contemplated that a moment. "And why wouldn't a pet live here?"

"Too many distractions."

"What does that mean?"

"It means dogs aren't stupid. They can see and hear things people can't." This was all coming together in my mind as I said this. To tell the truth, I was sort of thinking out loud.

Ma frowned again. "Are you really okay, Ryan?"

"I'm not the problem, Ma," I said, taking another long breath and trying—again—to organize my thoughts so I wouldn't sound like a babbling idiot. "Mantis is the problem. Mr. Mantis. Part of the problem, I mean, one of the problems."

"Well, I don't know what you're talking about, but I suppose we'll find out. I invited him and his wife over for dinner tonight."

Another brainlock: "You did what?"

"Sounds like fun," said Dad.

"Fun?" I almost yelled. "You guys aren't listening to me!"

"We are listening," said Dad, "and don't raise your voice. What is supposed to be the problem?"

"He thinks his teacher is a giant insect," said Anthony, coming into the room.

"What do you mean, giant insect?" asked Ma, taking her turn with the potatoes as she did. "You mean like Kafka?"

This time it was me who was confused. "Kafka? Kafka who?"

Ma explained. "Franz Kafka, he wrote a story

**88**

called 'Metamorphosis' where the main character wakes up in the morning changed into a giant cockroach."

"Not roach," I said. "More like a giant praying mantis or something. . . ."

She didn't even hear that because she was saying, "I remember something about his brother throwing an apple that stuck in his shell and killed him."

"I'm game," said Anthony.

I shot him a dirty look, then said to Ma, again, "Mantis."

"That's just his name."

"It's also a description."

"Well, he's bringing his wife," said Dad. "Is she supposed to be a bug, too?"

"I don't know what she's supposed to be. If she's not, she's in for a big shock someday."

"Ryan, what are you up to?"

"I'm not up to anything," I said.

"Well, you're not making a whole lot of sense."

"Nothing's made sense since we moved to this stupid town."

"Ahhh . . ." said Dad, finishing up with the potatoes now and getting ready to put them into the pan.

"Don't 'ahhh,' " I said. "There is no 'ahhh' here. My teacher is a bug—a giant horrible insect. You guys won't be able to see it, but I don't think it's good and I need some help."

My parents didn't address this. Instead Dad sort of shrugged, shot Ma a look, and then said to me, "Maybe you better just wait in your room until company comes. You've probably got homework to do, anyway."

Homework, I thought. Oh, yeah, there was an idea—I needed to find some way to get my family to see what I and the Wide-Awake Club kids could see. Remember, I kept telling myself, remember there's the wasp thing to keep in mind. Something obviously bad that made Terri Van Gelder cry and everybody else shut up.

Wasps. Read about the wasps, she had told me.

Fine. Grabbing the encyclopedia was first on the list.

Don't tell your parents anything, Patty had warned me. She was very serious all the times she said it, but that was probably that pheromone thing working against her, trying to keep her from letting the news spread any further. I'd seen those army trucks full of soldier bugs. If we couldn't convince the world what was going on, we were in big trouble, and the first people I needed to convince were my own family.

Preferably before the bugs arrived for dinner.

# 12

# Mmmmm, Mmmmm, Good

No. Please, please, please don't let it be true.

Again and again I closed my eyes, opened them, and read some more. It was always true.

I'd been reading about bugs in general, mantises what I could, and wasps.

Especially about wasps. And what I read wasn't good. It was scary—very scary.

Because wasps are parasites. The worst thing I read was the part that seemed to make the most sense. It was about a species of wasp that stings tarantulas, except it doesn't kill them. It merely stuns the tarantulas long enough to lay its wasp eggs inside the hairy spider's back.

Where they grow.

The spider recovers from the sting, gets up, and goes about his little spider life, never understanding what this growing lump on his back is, not until the little wasp eggs start hatching and the wasp larvae, baby wasps, begin eating him.

From the inside.

While he's still alive.

*Yeeeechh.*

Which got me to thinking about Mr. Mantis and not just Mr. Mantis, but all the fun goings-on in insect town. All the empty houses. All the talk of lumps.

By now you've figured out the horrible secret of Teddle, Texas. I had, anyway, and there was nothing Patty or her Wide-Awake Club or any of those weenies were going to do that would keep me quiet. Not anymore.

All those empty houses in town . . . all those people who supposedly had moved away. No way.

Teddle, Texas, was wasp food.

A big bowl of wasp Wheaties, and we were right smack in the middle of the milk.

Obviously, as this rant shows, I didn't have time to grasp or think about it because the downstairs doorbell was ringing, and there, at the door, was my teacher the bug, and with him was another bug who looked exactly as he did, except Mr. Mantis introduced it as his wife, "Trudy."

Trudy? Couldn't these impostor bugs come up with more real-sounding names?

"Trudy, hi," said Ma. Fortunately Trudy Mantis was holding a bowl in her hands, otherwise Ma would have gotten a handful of insect paw. Inside, Ma and the lady insect both giggled.

"Hello, Ryan," said Mr. Mantis, looking across the room at me.

I just stared back at him. "You have got to be kidding," I said.

Ma gave me an even worse look, then smiled back at this hideous insect couple. "Come on inside, please. It's so nice to finally have some company. We know so few people here in town. Just a few from my husband's job and, well . . ."

"I'm out at the base," said Dad.

"And can't talk about your job," nodded Mr. Mantis. "I understand completely."

They came into the living room, and as they did Mrs. Mantis handed Ma the bowl she was carrying. "A side dish to go with dinner."

"Oh, how nice," smiled Ma, pulling off the lid to take a look inside. Forget about the thought of being eaten alive by wasp larvae—this was the moment I almost passed out.

Seeing the inside of that bowl was worse than being stung. Maybe because it was like my brain was being stung. The bowl was full of bug food. Mantis food.

Other, smaller, deader bugs.

"It's sort of an old family recipe," said Mrs. Mantis, following Ma into the kitchen.

"Mmmm," said Mom. "It certainly smells delicious."

"Yeah, I'll try it," agreed Anthony from the stairs; he was on his way back down. "Of course, I'll try anything."

"So what do you do, Trudy? Are you a teacher, too?" Ma was asking all the normal questions.

"Oh no," said my teacher's bug wife. "I just sort of hang around the house."

"Killing flies?" I asked.

"Excuse me?" said the startled Mrs. Bug.

"Ignore him," said Ma. "He thinks he's trying to be funny."

Dad murmured to me, "Watch it guy. This is one of your teachers, after all."

"This dish smells so unusual," Ma was saying. "I can't wait to taste it. What did you say it was made from?"

I almost gagged. What was Mom saying? Why couldn't she see this stuff for what it was? Pheromones?

I shook my head to clear the image, but it was still there. There was no denying what Mom was about to serve for dinner, whether she meant to or not.

I followed into the dining room to get a better

look; Ma was putting the bowl down along with everything else that was on the set table. As always, Anthony was being rude, pouring himself a glass of iced tea without waiting, but that wasn't important. What was important was this: the huge glass serving dish was full of sauteed flies. Millions of them, in a gravy, and Mom was about to stick a big spoon in and taste it. . . .

"Ahhhh!" Without even planning ahead I let out a shriek and grabbed the tablecloth with all the strength I could and pulled. The balance of the entire table was offset, and everything went careening to the left with a huge crash as everyone jumped out of the way. Roast beef, potatoes, cranberry sauce, and sauteed houseflies crashed down together, completely inedible now, and I scrammed, running up the stairs.

The knock on the door took like all of a minute. It was Dad; he was pale and almost in a stuttering rage. "Have you lost your mind?"

"No, Dad, I . . ."

"Your mother is down there near tears. You just humiliated this entire family. Do you realize that?"

"Something really bad is happening, Dad."

"I just saw something really bad happen."

"No, I mean really bad. What's going on at the base, Dad? What are you doing out there?"

"Ryan, you know I can't talk about any of that. And don't change the subject."

"Can I have a minute?"

It was a new voice, in the hall, and Dad and I both looked at the same time.

In the doorway was Mr. Mantis, and even with my now-spinning brain there was no doubt about it. He was a bug, a six-foot-tall, twitching insect with antennae and a gaping maw, and he said, "Tom, let me talk to the boy a minute alone."

"No . . ." I started to say, "I don't want to," but I couldn't choke the words above a whisper because this bug-monster was in my room now, his shadow falling across me, and I felt like cowering under the bed in fear, and then Dad said the most terrible words in the history of all mankind: "Sure, maybe that'll help; I'll leave you two alone. . . ."

# 13

## MR. MANTIS

There he was. This was it.

Another big scene from all the stories like mine: the confrontation. The run-in between the good guy and the bad guy, where it all comes out in the wash. The time when the deepest, darkest secrets are brought out in the open.

Fine. I got right to business, whatever that business might be. "I know all about you," I told Mr. Mantis.

"I realize that," answered the bug.

So I stared at him. "Are you from another planet? Are you guys space aliens? Is that it?"

"From another planet? Yes. Space aliens? No."

"What does that mean?"

"We're from earth."

"You just said you weren't."

**97**

"We're not from this earth. We're from another earth, a parallel earth. Almost the same, but not quite, occupying the same space but in a different universe."

"That's not possible."

He just stared at me.

"Did you guys come in flying saucers?"

"Yes. But not at first."

He didn't say anything more about that.

"My head hurts," I said.

"I'm sorry," he said. "It's probably me causing that. I'm quite scared, and I'm probably giving off—"

"Pheromones?"

He was impressed. "You know about those?"

"I'm a regular expert these days," I said sarcastically. Then I realized what he'd said and asked, "Why would you be scared?"

"Because I'm not supposed to be telling you any of this."

"Then why are you?"

"Well, I don't hate humans. This is your world. You're exceptionally perceptive."

"It was the allergy medicine."

"I don't think so. Most of the town is on allergy medicine or something. That's where you've been mistaken. Pheromones aren't so easily beat as to be done in with pills. You can see because you're the type who always sees."

That felt sort of good to hear, even coming from a bug. "But why tell me?" I asked.

"You've a right to know."

"Yeah," I said.

"What can I do?" he asked.

"Do?"

"Yes."

"I don't know," I said. Then: "The wasps."

He nodded, or at least his head bobbed. "What do you know about the wasps?"

"I'm not sure," I said, picking up the encyclopedia. "I've heard some things from some people who are too scared to even think anymore."

"And you?"

"I'm getting more and more scared, but I can still think. These wasps, they're the reason all the people are disappearing from the town."

Mr. Mantis didn't answer at first, but then he nodded again. Sadly, I thought. "Yes."

A shudder ran through me. There it was.

"So what about you?" I asked.

This got to him, and he shook his head, saying, "No. No. We of the mantis race aren't like that— we don't have to be like that. We're not parasitic."

"Meaning?"

"It means our young don't have to live in the bodies of hosts."

Hosts. There was a suddenly hideous word.

"We don't breed like that," Mr. Mantis was saying.

"Oh no," I agreed. "I've been reading about you mantis types, too. The female kills the male."

Mr. Mantis seemed amused. "Not anymore. At least I hope not anymore."

"So what do you creepy bugs think?" I asked him. "Do you think we humans are going to just sit around and let you and your wasp buddies knock us off one by one, use our bodies to lay eggs in?"

"We and the wasps are not buddies."

"Why not? Aren't you all in on this together?"

"Not exactly."

"So what exactly?"

Mr. Mantis considered that. Then he said, "Until we found your human world, they were our enemies. Now there is a truce."

"Truce. Okay, go ahead and explain."

He did. Mr. Mantis said, "Where I come from, as in your world, there were once millions of different insect species. An almost infinite diversity. No longer. Where once there were millions, there are now only four. Four species, four races. That's all that's left."

"Ants, bees, wasps, and mantises," I said.

He nodded. "That's what you call them. A close approximation."

"What happened to the others?"

"Extinction. Natural and otherwise. Mostly otherwise. They were, over the millennium, killed off by those of us who survive."

"Nice."

"Not so nice," he said.

"So how did you bugs get over here? Why?"

"Do you know what a rift is?"

"No."

He explained, saying, "People walk through rifts all the time."

"People?"

Mr. Mantis crossed his antennae. I was beginning to realize that was his way of smiling when I said something he thought was funny. Or stupid. "People, the races. It gets confusing; I honestly think of us all as the same. Don't you consider me a person?" His antennae twitched.

"It's kind of hard to," I said. "After all, you do look like a bug."

"I am a bug. You're a mammal. It doesn't bother me that you strongly resemble a hedgehog."

"I do?"

**101**

"Nails, hair, teeth, warm-blooded. You're all the same, so what's the difference?"

"I wouldn't know."

"Of course not. So consider the problem. More than billions or trillions, an infinite number of parallel universes, stacked right on top of each other. Sort of like a color variation chart, each blending into the other. Light works that way; without some sort of prism you'd never see the differences. And each world is pretty much like the ones closest to it, but the farther you wander from one to another, the more alien to you the new worlds become."

"That's what happened to you guys?"

"That's what happens to all of us all the time. That's my point. Universal rifts, which are tears, tiny holes between worlds, are all over the place. I've been doing computations. Based on my research, each of us wanders from our world to an adjacent world, back and forth, to and fro, chancing on new alternatives. In this world you might end up driving a garbage truck, Ryan, but should you wander to the next you could become president. Changing your destiny simply means accidentally slipping yourself into the next world."

"Wow."

"Wow indeed. The only reason no one ever notices that they've wandered into a completely new world is because the ones closest to us, the ones we can get to, these are so close to our own as to be virtually identical. Oh, here and there a few odd, silly things are different. Ever experience what we call dèjá vu?"

"What's that?"

"It's when you go into a new place, or hear someone say something, and you have the odd feeling you've heard it or done it before, when you know you haven't."

"Yeah," I said. "The first time I went into my cousin's barn—they've got a farm up in Michigan—it was really weird, because I knew my way all around it, as if—"

"As if you'd seen the barn before. That's dèjá vu, and that's part of what I'm explaining to you. Cross-universal references."

"And you think that's what happened?"

"No. No matter what manner of mazes the rifts between the universes might concoct, I do not believe it possible to wander so far afield from home. This place is as alien to me as we are to you. This was no accident."

"You mean somebody brought you guys here on purpose?"

"Something like that. Someone was toying with barriers between the universes, and they've managed to connect to a version of the universe much farther, much more alien than they expected. And that's bad."

"Why bad?"

"It's bad, my young friend, because I and my kind do not represent the ones who rule where I come from. The wasps rule. And the bees. The ants. Those three powers once predicted by a great writer Jee-arge Errweel."

"What?"

Mr. Mantis nodded. "You have him here as well, save he was a human called George Orwell, and he wrote in his novel *1984* of a world where three future nations wage eternal war for the sheer futility of it. In my world this has happened; the wasps, bees, and ants fight each other solely to keep power. None of them even want to win; they just need an enemy to maintain their power and authority. But now . . . now some fool from your world out at that silly base has given them a new enemy to fight, a new world to conquer."

"No."

"Yes," said Mr. Mantis grimly. "Yours."

# 14

# THE FOOD CHAIN

Mr. Mantis and his wife went home, Dad stepped outside to switch on the lawn sprinklers, and everything was forgiven, supposedly, although Anthony made a point to whisper to me, "Nice going, dimwit," as I apologized to Ma.

I gave Anthony a glare, but that was when I noticed something about Ma. "Hey . . ."

"Yes, honey?"

A chill of dread was running across me, so I just came out and asked it: "What's wrong with your back?"

"With my back?" Ma sort of frowned at me as if she didn't fully understand what I was asking, yet at the same time she arched forward a bit. My words must have reminded her of how uncomfortable she was feeling.

"There's a lump in the center of your back. I can see it through your clothes. Are you all right?"

Ma gave me a weary smile. "I'm fine. Just a little tired—I've had a rough night."

"That's a fact," agreed Anthony.

"Are you sure?" I asked her again.

"Yes, I'm sure. I'm fine."

She wasn't fine. I knew that absolutely. She had one of those lumps, the kind Terri cried about and nobody else would talk about. My heart started pounding.

Not too late, I thought and thought again. Even Mr. Mantis the bug had said that to me—it wasn't too late.

I followed Anthony upstairs, but he wasn't going to hear any more weird talk. "This is serious, Anthony," I tried telling him. "Ma's sick. She's in trouble."

"You're a jerk, you know that? Of course you made her sick. You ruin dinner, and now who knows what you want to do?" With that he slipped on a pair of stereo headphones and tuned me out.

I did find Dad outside, still overseeing the yard, standing out by the curb and looking up and down the silent street. "Listen," he said.

I did. The only sound was the breeze shifting a

few leaves. Not even a slamming door or a running car motor to disturb this early hour of the night.

"No dogs," said Dad, as if just realizing what I'd told him so much earlier.

Not knowing whether or not I was supposed to, I didn't say anything. Dad looked around some more, then, still without looking at me, he said, "Ryan. These bugs you say you see . . ."

"Yeah?"

"Where are they supposed to come from? Outer space?"

"I don't know," I said at first. Then, remembering Mr. Mantis's confession, I said, "No. Another version of here, of earth. From out in the desert."

"Out at the base," Dad finished, as if he were nowhere near finished.

"Yeah," I said again, waiting. Waiting some more.

"I . . ." Dad started to speak, and very nearly said something that would have been the envy of the man in black, but he changed his mind. Dad was always careful, always honest. He didn't talk about the base; he didn't talk about his work. So all he said was, "Let's get inside. It's getting late. . . ."

It was getting later than anyone thought.

I ran into Patty early at school. Her eyes were

**107**

bright and she was smiling, but as soon as I told her about Ma she tried tuning me out. "You can't talk about that," she said.

"I am talking about it," I said, angry now. I couldn't believe how ready I was to explode. "My mother is not about to become one of the major food groups, okay?"

"It's not okay," she said. "You don't understand what could happen by talking about it."

"It? It? Listen to yourself," I said. "I'm about to get real loud talking about it. This stuff isn't so secret anymore, you know. Mr. Mantis was at my house last night, and he was talking about it. So you and the Wide-Awake Club should change your name to the Sound Asleep Club or the Kids-with-Their-Heads-in-the-Sandbox Club."

Patty's eyes went wide, disbelieving. "Mr. Mantis was at your house? He told you what he was?"

"How could he not tell me? I'm not blind; nobody has to be blind. He told me about the wasps. He told me that it was up to us to do something about it. It's our world. Let's fight for it."

Patty pulled away. "You don't know what you're talking about."

"I do know what I'm talking about. I'm talking to Quint, Vic, Terri, whomever."

"We don't have time for this stuff right now," she said. "We have to go to school."

**108**

It was my turn to stare in disbelief, and I shook my head, calling after her. "School's out, Ms. Patricia."

Except it wasn't, except maybe for me, and I had an action plan, or so I thought. There was another assembly scheduled, and it wasn't so hard to figure out what that was all about. Another feisty bit of brainwashing at the hands of the buzz-buzz crowd, or maybe worse. I decided to skip it, and so did Mr. Mantis. We got away with it by his escorting me back to the science classroom.

"They got my mom," I told him, with no huffing or puffing because I wanted a straight answer.

He had been fluttering around a supply cabinet and turned. "What do you mean 'got her'?"

"You know what I mean. She's got that back thing, the lump. The wasp thing."

The great insect teacher actually twitched.

I asked the question that had to be asked, scary as it was. "Will she die?"

"Not if the larvae are removed." Mr. Mantis opened the cabinet now, going through the things at the bottom, looking for something hidden back there.

"Really? How do we do that?"

"A doctor could do it. A human doctor."

"Not in this town."

"That's true," he agreed. Mr. Mantis produced what he had been looking for—a silver ball, just about the size of a baseball, except when he touched something on it the ball began pulsating, breathing. Blowing up and out, to the size of a soccer ball, and then becoming smaller again, then blowing big again.

"This is the key," he said.

"The key. It looks like a metal beach ball."

"It is the key," he said. "This shimmering ball is what I've been modifying, toying with. This is what opens the door so one may travel from world to world without a cynget."

"Cynget," I said. "Is that a . . ."

"What you would call a flying saucer, yes. Cyngets can travel between the worlds or between the stars—except that takes a lot longer. So I'm told."

"Terrific."

"If not for the experiments at Teddle Base, our cyngets could never have found your world. Even in this world they remain fragile. So we started using keys."

"Lots of bugs have those?"

"Not like this one," said Mr. Mantis, confident now. "This one has several modifications."

"What's so special about that one?"

"It wouldn't be enough for my wife and me to escape back to our world—not if this doorway between worlds remains open, not if the wasps, ants, bees are free to roam back and forth. My race would still be slaves to them there. But now there is an opportunity. Most of the armies are moving about, to this world and others."

"Yeah? And?"

"Well, this key not only gives us the power to get back home to our world, but it affects the doorway itself. When the others attempt to return they will find the path blocked, changed toward those worlds where other ants, other bees, other wasps continue to slaughter each other."

"You mean . . ."

"Yes. This key locks the door."

"That'll work," I said as I watched him switch off and tuck the silver ball back away. But then, still distracted by my own problems, I reminded him that I had been stung by that bee guard. "What was that all about? Have I been . . . uh, infected, too?" I tried to reach back behind myself and feel for a lump but couldn't manage.

"You're safe enough for now," said Mr. Mantis. "You're big for your age but not mature enough to be a host body. Only adult humans have the strength and," he said with some disgust, "the

**111**

wasps care too much for their young to risk them on immature hosts."

"Wonderful," I said. Then, even though I already knew, I asked, "What happens to my mother when they hatch?"

He didn't answer.

"What about the rest of us?"

"Eventually all the adult humans will be wasp hosts. The children won't be safe, of course. Newly hatched wasps are ravenous, starving. And very, very fast."

"Yuck."

"Survival of the species," he said. "That's how they breed. That's how they kept up the struggle against the superior numbers of the bees and the ants."

"And you guys, the mantis types."

"We're intellectuals."

"Right."

Mr. Mantis gave me a grim look that I could have sworn was a smile. "Welcome back to the bottom of the food chain, human. . . ."

# 15

# INVISIBLE MAZES

"It is so very important that you trust me," Mr. Mantis said after a long while. The subject was door location and why we couldn't just toss down his hidden metal ball wherever we wanted; it could only be done in certain locations. Which confused me, of course, but this was nothing new. Mr. Mantis was explaining to me things that I could never have understood, although he kept insisting, "Try, try."

"Try?" I asked. Mantis was at the blackboard, whipping through math formulas like this was a college lecture. "Why are you even bothering with that? I can't even follow the simple parts, and there are no simple parts."

"I think better with math," he said. "Math is the only truly universal language."

"Terrific. I'll remember that the next time a Russian kid comes over to my house; we'll do times tables together."

"You must understand the bottom line of what I am trying to teach you. Perhaps not all of it, but its importance—the basic concepts."

"Why?"

"Because you don't need to know how to build a car in order to drive one, but it helps if you know enough to open and close the door and work the key in the ignition." Mr. Mantis was firm, annoyed.

"Right," I said.

"And there is more," he said, both antennae standing firm and tall now, his never-seen beetle wings quivering beneath his suit-coat jacket.

"What more?"

"Because together, you and I are the only ones who might be able to prevent this thing from happening. You've looked around; you know how many invaders are in your world already. The only thing we've got going for us is the fact that the wasps, bees, and ants distrust each other so much that they're all sending their forces across just a few at a time. They don't want to risk being outnumbered by the others, here or at home."

I considered this a moment. "So what are we going to do?"

"I have a plan, but it is risky."

"What do you mean?"

Again he took what for a human would have been a deep breath, but on him just made those tucked-away wings rattle. "If we're able to get onto the base, into the rift alignment area before they start to arrive, I can derail the thing—send them somewhere else."

"What? You mean just zap some other poor world with an army of invading insects?"

"Yes, but they'll be in for an unpleasant surprise. As I said, the world I have in mind for them is populated almost entirely by others of their own kind, a world where the warring wasps, bees, and ants have managed to do in all but themselves. They deserve each other."

"Cool," I said, but then something else occurred to me. "But what about you guys?"

"Once the majority of the warriors are lost for all eternity we—the intellectuals—should be able to make our own world. We'll return home via the portal. But somebody's going to have to hold open the door and close it behind us."

"Me," I thought.

"Yes," agreed Dr. Mantis, speaking my thoughts right out loud. "You."

"You're in a lot of trouble, Mantis."

That was an interruption, and we both turned:

**115**

it was Patty. We watched her come into the classroom, except she wasn't alone. With her was that wasp principal, Mr. Nader—or whatever his real name was—and two bee guards with those stinger-sticks.

"Kneel before me, Mantis," buzzed Nader-Wasp, in all his Roman soldier glory. "For you are a traitor to our races."

"Not my race," said Mr. Mantis, making no move to kneel. "The humans have as much right to their world as we do to ours."

"We have rights to all worlds, all worlds," said Nader-Wasp. "Their fortune is to be our slaves. Our food. It is their destiny."

"They may prove tougher to defeat than you think, Nadd-Irr."

The scary wasp guy buzzed, but I caught this much: "I think not."

That end of what was happening in the class wasn't my major concern: Ms. Patricia was. More than a little bit shocked, I couldn't believe it. "You're with them?" I asked Patty.

"They're my family," she said.

"Say what? You mean you're a bug?"

"No. I'm human, but . . ."

"But what?"

She seemed to take a moment to remember. "Once I knew exactly who I was. Now I don't know. All I know is what I've been taught since that day I was taken—somewhere—and left on that empty road outside of Teddle."

"Now I'm lost," I said.

"No," said Patty. "I was the one who was lost, until that cop found me and brought me out to the base. Except they knew me already there, and they couldn't be sure everything was right and they got rid of him. They took me, and they brought me back, and I didn't remember or know much but . . ." Her eyes twinkled now. "I knew what a cynget was."

"So do I," I said. "But how does a ride on a flying saucer make you into one of them?"

"Not one of them. One with them."

"But you changed sides. You're a traitor."

"Not a traitor," said Patty, pausing for a thoughtful moment before going on. "A survivor. Humans are going extinct, aren't they, Mr. Mantis? You said so yourself in class, lots of times. Insects are the survivors. They're the ones who are going to be around after the end of the world. Well, I want to be around, too."

I still couldn't believe I was hearing this. How could a person turn on the whole human race? "You'd give up people to these wasp guys?"

"At least I won't wind up with a wasp using my body for food," she said cruelly.

**117**

"They don't need your body," I told her as we were led away. "They've already got your soul."

The truth about Patty wasn't so difficult to understand, although I didn't realize it all at the time, nor would I have had the time to think about it, anyway. The man in black was on that case already. He knew where she had been, what had happened to her—or at least he had enough clues to fake his way through it.

There was an army truck outside of the school, brought out from the base, and Mr. Mantis and I were taken away.

I was much calmer about the whole thing than should have been possible, but then again, maybe I was beyond shock. In Teddle, Texas, what could be shocking?

"I've known about this a lot longer than I let on to you before," she told me on the ride out to whatever was going to happen to us. "It wasn't falling into a swimming pool that set my brain."

"What?"

Patty had been to the other side—on a cynget—on a flying saucer. The bugs had brainwashed her, set her for control, and brought her back. Not just to watch other humans, but to

**118**

watch traitor bugs, or bugs that might turn traitor while living among the humans.

Bugs like Mr. Mantis.

They took us to the base and threw us in cells next to each other in the stockade; the bugs were in complete control and now they were starting to round up their enemies.

It was a long hallway of cells, the light wasn't great, but I wasn't alone because in my cell were Terri and Vic and most of the other members of the so-called Wide-Awake Club, except Quint. I asked Vic where he was.

"Bugs didn't get him yet," Vic answered.

"That's good, I guess."

"We'll be okay, though," said Terri, trembling. "Daddy knows. Daddy knows."

"What?"

"Daddy knows. He's got guns. He'll do something."

Nobody else was popping off, so I asked Vic if he knew what she was talking about.

Vic shrugged. "Terri says she got her dad to believe her. He's supposedly one of the big military base honchos." Vic looked sympathetic, but he didn't look like he believed any rescue was on the way.

I didn't, either. In the cell I had a little while

**119**

to think, and finally I just went ahead and asked Mr. Mantis the real question, the one that had been bugging me for so long. "Listen," I said. "If you mantis types are such intellectuals, why did you go along with all this? With all this killing and invading and stuff? Why didn't you guys say no?"

Mr. Mantis seemed embarrassed, maybe, but finally he did answer, and it was so obvious that I felt stupid. "The same reason Patty and others did. We can be used to feed baby wasps, too. . . ."

# 16

# THE BATTLE OF TEDDLE

So I got to sit in the adjoining cell next to my old teacher the bug and chat while the wasp guys decided what they were going to do to us. Terri was sure her father would save her, "Especially with Quint out there to get them going," but Vic and I didn't find much comfort in that argument.

Instead we talked to Mr. Mantis, who occupied the cell across from us. Vic was impressed with how relaxed and easygoing I was, talking with bugs. "So, how are we going to get you out of here now?"

"We still need the key," he reminded me.

"So why did you guys stop going by flying saucer?"

"Cynget," he corrected me. "Flying saucer sounds so . . . so tacky."

"Whatever. So what happened to them?"

As always, he gave a thoughtful pause before answering. "The cyngets—the ships—they crashed a lot. It took a long while to deduce why. Not all the laws of physics apply in both universes; nothing worked exactly right."

"And they crash over here?"

"They crash often enough to give one a fear of flying."

"I hear that," I said. "So what about this universal door knocker you're talking about?"

"I was modifying mine," he said, "against all the rules."

"Trying to help everybody, eh?"

"I thought so."

He was moping more than I was. "What's really wrong?" I asked him. In answer he simply shrugged and confessed: "I'm worried about my wife."

"So she is really your wife?"

"Yes."

"Is her name really Trudy?"

His antennae crisscrossed. "No. But you couldn't pronounce her real name."

"Probably not," I agreed. "I can't even pronounce Massachusetts."

He crossed those antennae again.

One thing was for sure: "We won't be closing any universal rifts, will we, Mr. Mantis?"

"Indeed," he agreed. "It doesn't seem like it. Our prospects seem grim."

Fortunately, for the first time, my teacher the bug was wrong.

I was the first one to hear a noise.

Whether it was that distant buzzing becoming that wasp noise or the rifle shots I heard first, who knows. But almost immediately there was a roar and a lot of yelling, and it was just like the old movies where the townspeople storm the monster's castle to set the prisoners free, because that's exactly what was happening.

Terri was right.

"Hey," said Vic, rising from the bunk in the cell. A couple of the others started to get up, too, but the stockade was already under attack by then. A rescue! Terri Van Gelder's old man was busting his way in.

And one of the guys with them was Dad!

It wasn't just Dad and the other guys who worked at the base, because also with them was my brother, Anthony.

Still, I couldn't believe we were being rescued. How could they have even known? "I don't understand."

Anthony looked a little sheepish but held up

**123**

his stereo headphones, the ones he'd been listening to the night before. "I had your room bugged, my tape recorder under your bed. I thought you were going to get chewed out and I wanted to laugh. But I accidentally taped your talk with Mr. Mantis."

"And you played it for Dad?"

"Yeah. And Ma. They thought I was crazy until they checked out Ma's back. And talked to some other people."

"Everybody, we're leaving," announced Dad.

I looked across the hall at Mr. Mantis sitting sadly in his cell. "What about him?" I asked Dad.

"You mean 'it'? He's one of them."

"He's not a wasp."

"He's a bug."

"He's one of the good bugs."

"They're all the same."

"Nothing and nobody are ever all the same, Dad. Come on, we can't leave him here. They'll kill him."

It took Dad a moment to make up his mind, and he nodded. Mr. Van Gelder had the keys and he worked the lock, a little nervous. "He's not going to bite me, is he?"

"Not likely."

My teacher the bug looked at me and said thanks.

Meanwhile, alarm bells were still going off. "We need to get out of here," said Dad. "Any time now would be good."

"Right," agreed Mr. Van Gelder, cocking back his rifle.

"The key," my insect friend murmured to me.

"I know, I know," I said.

"These wasps are just about out of control," complained Mr. Van Gelder. "How many are too many, though? We got through the ones on guard before the alarms went off, but now . . . who knows?"

"Aren't there any human soldiers left?" I asked. "How come they're not defending the place?"

"The transition was very quick," said Mr. Mantis. "But we will be able to move. The wasps are very fast and deadly, but they're also very fragile."

"I'm not real sure where to go, where we are right now," said Dad. "Out at the lab we never had access to the general areas of the base. Now we know why."

That buzzing noise was louder now, reverberating throughout the building. "We don't have much of a chance, do we?"

"Not much," said Dad. "But we still need to try, don't we?"

"Yeah," I said, picking up a flyswatter that just

happened to be lying on a nearby desk. "We're not about to let these bugs ruin us." I looked at Mr. Mantis and added, "No offense."

"None taken."

"Let's go," said Dad.

We moved out of the building, into the daylight, and the buzzing and screaming out there was incredible. Our first stop was to duck behind the rear of a parked army truck for cover; the front doors were open, and a zapped wasp lay smashed against the inside of the windshield.

"That's a first," said Dad.

Our old buddy Nader-Wasp was out there, leading the insect army, buzzing waspish threats like, "All humans will feed our young," but with Dad, Anthony, and Mr. Van Gelder zapping them with machine guns it didn't seem so scary. At least not until we started to run out of bullets.

"This isn't good," said Dad. "I've only got fifteen rounds left."

"You guys are shooting too fast," said Mr. Van Gelder, cursing himself for working with amateurs, I guess. "Only fire when you can see the whites of their eyes."

"What whites? What eyes?" asked Anthony.

"You know what I mean."

That, of course, would have been exactly what the wasp army wanted. The bugs believed in up-

**126**

close fighting; it was almost like an old sword fight movie, except the bugs' swords all had poison in them, and I didn't think anyone was going to be dragged to the nurse's office today. Our advantage, though, was people didn't fight that way—except when they were running out of ammunition. Mr. Van Gelder was using his machine gun to keep the wasps at bay and he said, "Go ahead and climb in the back of the truck. I'll cover you."

We did; Dad and Mr. Van Gelder got to the front, climbed in, and started the engine. Anthony was shooting from the back, keeping the bad guys—bad bugs—away, and the truck lurched into gear.

Mr. Mantis touched my arm. "I need to get away, on my own," he said as we rammed through the main gate and raced into town, pursued by crazed bugs.

"What? Are you nuts?"

"The key, remember? I have to get back to the school and find the key."

"Right," I said, remembering. "I can't go with you; I need to help my mom."

"I understand," he said. "Take care." Mr. Mantis crawled up, leaned over the edge, and leaped from the speeding truck, rolling and bouncing. I looked to see if he was hurt, but he was up and scurrying away; I don't think the wasps even saw him.

Our truck roared down the dusty road.

Behind us, the base alert signals were ringing everywhere, and gunfire and buzzing and shrieks were all over. "Pretty intense, eh?" asked Anthony.

"Yeah."

A moment later the truck slammed to a halt, the front doors opened, and Mr. Van Gelder yelled, "Down! Get down! Roadblock!"

It was true. A bee patrol had the road to downtown blocked up ahead, and Anthony and I crouched beside Dad as Mr. Van Gelder tried to come up with another escape plan. "Where's your pet bug?" he asked.

"Gone."

"Ran out on us, eh? Figures."

He didn't run out, I thought, but I said nothing. I wasn't feeling brave, but I wasn't as scared as I should have been, either. Why not? I was fast on my feet, remember. All we had to do was get out of there, get back to Ma, and get clear of that town.

Get to the real world.

Warn people, before it was too late.

Then yet another miracle took place.

"Look!" yelled Anthony, pointing to the sky.

We all did. At first my heart almost popped because I thought the sky was full of buzzing wasps and bees swooping down on the base and all of us, but then I realized they were parachutes—hundreds and hundreds of parachutes falling from planes in the sky.

It was a war of the worlds, and my side was finally showing up.

"Hooray!" Mr. Van Gelder was screaming at the top of his lungs. "The cavalry is coming!"

"That's not cavalry," said Dad. "More like United States Marines!"

"Whatever," I said to everybody. "Just so long as they're not afraid of wasps."

So began the real Battle of Teddle. Where was Patty? I wondered then. What would they do to her? How would people punish her for changing sides like she had?

Who knows? What I really didn't know then was I was about to change sides myself.

# 17

# COLONEL FINCH

The Battle of Teddle itself didn't last so long, but
the chaos that followed did. Night was falling and
the town was sealed off from the outside world,
and soldiers were going from house to house
rounding up bugs. Most of the mantis types
didn't put up a fight, but the wasps, bees, and
ants did, and that was taking up most of the
soldiers' time.

The guy in charge of the soldiers was a marine
colonel named Finch, and I got to talk to him
because along with Dad I was with the base people who were questioned. There was a military
field hospital being set up by helicopter. A team
of doctors and medics were working to help all
the people the wasps had attacked. Ma was one
of them. The operation wasn't that serious—the

wasp eggs hadn't grown much—and the medic said there wouldn't be much of a scar.

I was looking around for Patty. What was her status? In a weird way I wasn't even mad at her. What was this little cynget trip she'd been taken on? The amnesia, all the rest of it? What horrible things had they done to her to make her work for them?

Dad had his own questions. "How did your people know what was going on?" he asked the colonel.

"Orders from higher up," said the colonel, securing the radio headset he had been speaking on. "Way high up."

"How way?" asked Anthony. "From the president?"

"Higher than that," answered the colonel. "Let's just say there are little fire alarm boxes around the government for special fires, and somebody real special pulled the switch."

*The man in black,* I thought, remembering the weird guy I had seen from before. It was just a hunch, though; I had no reason to be thinking it.

The colonel just shrugged. "Weird as the orders were, we didn't question them, and our orders were simple: take back Teddle Base. Take back Teddle."

"Take it back from the bugs."

Colonel Finch shrugged again. "Bugs, aliens, martians, Russians, whatever. Doesn't matter to me or my men. We're soldiers."

"But how did you know what was really going on here?" Mr. Van Gelder kept asking.

"Who knows?" said the colonel. "I already told you. Probably one of those men in black. . . ."

I knew it!

"What men in black?" I asked, following the colonel. How did I know? Who was that guy I saw?

"Never mind, forget I said that. We've got mopping up to do around here."

Across the street I saw a camouflaged soldier leading a pair of mantis types up the block at rifle point. Then I recognized one of them: it was my Mr. Mantis.

They hadn't gotten away.

"What's going to happen to them?" I asked, running after the colonel again.

"Same thing that should happen to all bugs," he answered. "Extermination."

"You mean you're going to kill all the bugs?"

"Not for me to say."

"But they're not like regular bugs."

"Yeah. They're worse, more dangerous."

"They come from another world."

"That was their first mistake."

Colonel Finch was not a man to be reasoned with.

I was beginning to feel sorry that I'd ever told my story to the man, because Colonel Finch was only remembering the bad parts and not all the other stuff I had told him later. He wanted to kill all the bugs—all of them—and he didn't care what their stories might be.

And Mr. and Mrs. Mantis were in an awful lot of trouble. Maybe a lot of it was their fault, but a lot of it definitely wasn't.

I decided to do something if I could.

"This is like an infection, son," said the colonel very solemnly. "One must exterminate it before it spreads."

"But what if they're not all bad?" I asked. "What if some of them are sort of good?"

"They are invaders, son," said the colonel. "How can they possibly be good?"

He ignored me then, barking orders to his soldiers. "We're going to have to secure this place for the night," Colonel Finch said. "We should be locked-up tight by midday tomorrow, but I want everybody playing it safe tonight. It's getting dark, and there's a lot of wasps out there."

I didn't have time to come up with a good plan, so I went with a bad one. I told Anthony to keep an eye on Ma and Dad; I'd be back.

"Where are you going?" he asked.

"Gotta help somebody," I said.

So I took off, stopped real quick at the abandoned drug store, found what I needed, and ran down the street and over to the soldier who was guarding Mr. and Mrs. Mantis. "Colonel needs to see you, fast."

"What?"

"He said now. No questions."

The soldier looked around for a better answer, couldn't find one, and asked me, "What about these bugs?"

I held up my gun. It was only a squirt gun I got at the drug store, but he couldn't tell that in the dark. "I've got them," I said.

So I did. The goofy soldier ran off to find his colonel and now I had my teacher the bug and his wife. "We don't have much time," I said.

"That's for sure," he agreed.

"We need to get to the school. Get your key."

"We're in luck," said Mr. Mantis, patting the pocket of his jacket. "We had already claimed it before the soldiers got us."

"Great." We got away in the turmoil and made our way out into the desert, which probably wasn't the brightest idea since we had no water or supplies, but it was dark and the only light was now from the full moon. They both looked tired, if a giant green bug can look tired.

We wandered deep into the base and cut our way through a fence with some wire cutters— something else Mr. Mantis had in his pocket. "This is weird," I said, "breaking into a base."

"You don't have to go any farther, Ryan," said Mr. Mantis. "You've done more than enough. Thank you."

"I'm with you a while longer," I said. "I want to make sure you guys get through this doorway you're talking about."

"We may not make it," Mr. Mantis suggested. In the distance noises were becoming audible, and it wasn't difficult to figure out what they were. Helicopters. Search parties.

"Will they find us soon?" I asked.

"Just a little farther," said my teacher the bug. "It has to be the right vector into the parallel."

"Whatever that means," I said, listening to the closing choppers. "Better hurry."

We walked for another ten minutes or so, ducking as aircraft zoomed over and around above us. Occasionally a spotlight would zap the earth, but they didn't see us. Not yet. "They're using infrared, I'm sure," said Mr. Mantis, "but that won't do much for us. Insect body temperatures aren't so high, and you're shivering in the cold."

"Just a little," I admitted.

"Here," Mr. Mantis finally said. We stopped

**135**

and he pulled the small metal ball from his pocket. "The soldier never even searched me," he explained.

Then he threw a switch on it, and it started to pulsate again, growing bigger and smaller. Breathing. "Looks like a magic soccer ball," I said.

"It almost is," he said, rolling the ball on the ground, toward me. "Give it a kick."

"What?"

"Go on. Kick it—as hard as you can."

"It looks like metal; I'll bust my foot."

"You'll be fine. Go on."

"Yes," said Mrs. Mantis, finally speaking. "Go ahead, please."

I shrugged. "Whatever works," I said, and I ran up and really whopped it.

Part of the world exploded.

The ball didn't fly—it sparked, a shower of blue, then red, then white light that turned into a sliver of light that crept up from the ground until it was six feet high, the size of a door. The screech it made was deafening.

"Cool!" I yelled.

"Watch," cautioned my teacher the bug. I did. It was like the light peeking around a door frame, and then the door itself opened.

The door to another world.

Above us, helicopters were swarming, getting closer. The light from the doorway was blinding. "There's the path," I said.

"Yes," Mr. Mantis yelled back. "Now is the time. We'll go now."

I knew he was right, but I still felt bad. "Good luck!" I yelled.

"Good luck right back!" he replied. Then he grabbed his wife, and together they disappeared into the brightness. A moment passed and so did the light.

Everything was black there in that field, but only for a second because I was then caught in another bright light, except this one was from above. For a flash my heart jumped because I was thinking cynget—you know, one of those flying saucers, but then the whup-whup-whup noise overwhelmed me as well, and I realized it was just a helicopter.

Just a bunch of helicopters, their spotlights all training down on me.

"Do not move!" screamed Colonel Finch's voice over the public address system. "Raise your hands up over your head!"

I did. What else was I supposed to do?

Beyond the fringe of the light I now saw a circle of green-clad soldiers closing in on me. Human soldiers. It beat the other choice, I

**137**

thought, but I figured my life was about to make another turn for the worse.

Then another figure stepped into the light with me. The man in black. Together with me in the harsh white light, he seemed so pale as to be washed out, drained of all color. He looked up at the circling helicopters—there were at least three—and waved:

They all flew away; even the soldiers were retreating into their tracks, leaving me and the man in black all alone in that dark desert night. . . .

# 18

## ENCOUNTERS

There he was, the man in black, the source and answer for all the mysteries—or so I was to discover—and he was standing across from me in the desert with this fairly satisfied look on his face. The first thing he said to me, after all the Teddle business and who knew what else, was this: "I'm hungry. Are you hungry? Let's get something to eat."

So we did.

"We've been getting ready to meet for a long time," said the man in black.

"Yeah? So what happens now?"

He shrugged. "Nothing. What did you think was supposed to happen? Did your friends make it back to their home safely?"

"I don't know. I think so."

He considered it. "I think so, too. I know a bit about these things. They weren't the problem, anyway."

"What was the problem?"

"This world's got a million, zillion weird problems, son," said the man in black. "What's a problem for one town is hardly ever a problem for another. In Teddle it was bugs, and we took care of that. In some places the problem is Bigfoot, or the Loch Ness Monster, or aliens from space. Here it was bugs. We took care of it."

"You took care of it."

"We did. I did my part. I'm just an all-American kind of guy," he said.

Finally, I asked him just who the heck he was. To my surprise, he actually answered, telling me the whole story, even though it took hours, as we sat there eating breakfast at the Teddle Truck Stop, which never closed—even for bug infestations.

"How did this whole thing start?" I asked.

"How did it all start? Or just the Teddle part?"

"I don't know. All of it, I guess."

"Well," he said, in his easygoing way, "most of it is sort of classified."

"So what does that mean?"

"It means I can only tell you what the tabloid

papers would tell you. Which means the whole thing started with some airline pilots who thought they saw a demon flying through the sky."

"And?"

"And I think you know what they really saw— a very ticked off wasp. Which wasn't a surprise, another very classified top-secret fact you can read about is that flying saucers crash all the time."

"Cyngets."

"Eh?"

"Flying saucers are called cyngets."

"That's one name for them, anyway," he admitted.

"What are some others?"

"That's classified. Read about it in the papers."

That was a frustrating answer. "If this stuff is so classified, how can I read about it in the supermarket papers?"

"You tell me."

"Come on. . . ."

The man in black smiled, he actually smiled. "Ever wonder why flying saucers can supposedly travel millions of miles and then always seem to crash in Nevada or Texas? Ever wonder why they never kidnap a scientist, why it's always some fool who can hardly tie their own shoelaces? Ever wonder why UFOs always seem to be so, well, preoccupied? They don't even stop and say hello. Ever wonder about all that?"

"Yeah."

"So do I. That's my job. It's a good job."

"And the answers are?"

"That's classified."

"So I need to go read about it."

"Exactly."

"You're making me crazy."

"I'm just a guy."

Just a guy, I thought. Just a guy in black. "Okay," I said, "so I know about Teddle."

"Teddle," he said. "The place where cyngets chased away the real flying saucers."

"Say what?"

"Sorry. Can't talk about that. It's—"

"Classified. Read about it."

"Right."

This nonsense went on and on for hours, the man in black seeming to get a good laugh out of it all. Finally he wound down, saying, "The government is so big that any one part never knows what the rest is up to, and some parts are so secret that nobody else knows anything about them. Like my part."

I nodded.

So the man in black started to get up and walk

away, but first he said, "So forget all about me. What do you say?"

"I can't do that."

"Probably not," he agreed after some more thought. "You're a perceptive person."

"I just heard that from a bug."

"Whoever, whatever. Truth is truth." He thought some more. "After all this I suppose you could believe in almost anything."

"I don't know," I said, considering it. "Does it matter?"

He shrugged. "It might. To a future man in black."

That caught me off guard, and I thought about what he was saying. "You mean like you? I could be a guy like you?"

"I didn't say that. You don't even know what I really am. I don't even exist. But you could be your own man. There's always a place for a guy who's his own man."

I nodded.

"Anyway," he said, "if you have to tell your story, just keep it straight. Tell it all honestly."

"You mean I can tell? I won't get thrown in jail or bumped off or anything else?"

The man in black shook his head. "Nah, why would we bother? Nobody will believe you, anyway. Just another bit of classified information."

"That we all get to read about."

"Right."

Which is probably true.

The man in black left it at that. He paid for breakfast, dropped me off at home, and I haven't seen him since.

Anyway, all that's behind us now, except for one thing, which bothers me, but I don't know whether it's good or bad or what to do about it. It's going to be taken care of, I keep telling myself. The man in black—maybe men in black— are scurrying around out there in the country, the world, and they're on to all the weird stuff afoot. All of it. I'm certainly not up to it myself.

Not yet, anyway.

The thing of it is this. . . .

The other day I was watching television, flicking through the TV channels, and I saw the president on Channel 7 giving a speech before Congress, and the camera panned around to all the people in the Congress and Senate, and they were applauding and stuff.

Problem: some of them were bugs.

Answer? Here we go again.

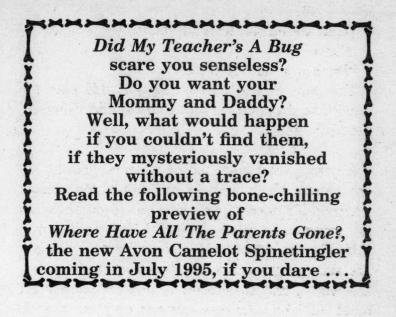

*Did My Teacher's A Bug*
scare you senseless?
Do you want your
Mommy and Daddy?
Well, what would happen
if you couldn't find them,
if they mysteriously vanished
without a trace?
Read the following bone-chilling
preview of
*Where Have All The Parents Gone?*,
the new Avon Camelot Spinetingler
coming in July 1995, if you dare . . .

Whatever it was had a huge head and two huge eyes, and it was coming toward me, saying, "I want your brain! I need your brain!"

"No!" I screamed.

I turned and tried to run, but my feet wouldn't move.

"I want your brain!" the thing kept saying. "I need your brain!"

Far away, I could hear a ringing sound. Someone was at our front door. "Help me!" I cried. "Help me!"

The thing was getting closer now. "I want your brain! I need your brain!"

Suddenly, the ground gave way, and I fell into blackness, hitting bottom with a thud.

"Ouch!"

I opened my eyes. It took a minute to realize that I was on the floor in my room, tangled up in my sheets. I had fallen out of bed.

It had all been a bad dream.

Downstairs, I could still hear the ringing, but it was the telephone, not the doorbell.

I lay there for several seconds, trying to come to grips with what had just happened to me, wishing, too, that either Mom or Dad would answer the stupid telephone, because the ringing was getting on my nerves.

If I had a phone in my room, I could answer it, but no, my parents decided I could use the ones in the kitchen or the den until I got to high school. The one in their bedroom was off-limits.

The telephone continued ringing.

"I'd answer the phone if it were in my room!" I screamed, still struggling to free myself from the sheets.

Finally, I was able to stand up. I went to the door and shouted, "Mom, Dad, answer the telephone!"

Still it continued to ring.

Now, I was more puzzled than irritated. "Mom? Dad?" I ran downstairs to the kitchen and grabbed the receiver. "Hello!"

"What took you so long, Mary?" It was my best friend, Pattie Chambers.

"I thought my parents would get it. Usually, the slightest noise wakes them up."

"Are they there?"

"Is who here?"

"Your parents. Are they there?"

"Of course they're here, Pattie. Why wouldn't they be?"

"Mine aren't. I got up this morning, and they weren't anywhere around."

"Hold on, then. I'll go check."

I put down the receiver and ran toward my parents' bedroom, which is on the first floor of our house. The door was open, which surprised me, so I didn't have to knock. There was no one in bed, although I could tell it had been slept in.

"Mom? Dad?"

No answer. It was weird.

I ran frantically from room to room, flinging open doors and calling them. I even looked in the garage. Now I was really getting scared.

Then I raced upstairs, where I did the same thing. My parents weren't anywhere in the house.

Downstairs again, I looked out the kitchen window to see if they were in the backyard. They weren't. They weren't in the front yard, either.

**149**

I ran back to the telephone. "No, Pattie, my parents aren't here, either, and they didn't leave me a note saying they went somewhere." Even as I said it, I knew they wouldn't have done anything like that. Something was really wrong.

# IF YOU DARE TO BE SCARED...
# READ SPINETINGLERS!

## *by* M.T. COFFIN

### THE SUBSTITUTE CREATURE
**77829-7/$3.50 US/$4.50 Can**

Everyone knows about substitute teachers. When they show up it's time for fun and games. That's why no one believes Jace's crazy story about seeing the new substitute, Mr. Hiss, in the men's room...smearing blood all over his hands and face!

### BILLY BAKER'S DOG WON'T STAY BURIED
**77742-8/$3.50 US/$4.50 Can**

Billy Baker's dog Howard has come back from the dead...bringing all his friends from the pet cemetery. Every night, long-dead cats and dogs dig themselves out of their graves in search of people who bullied and beat them, locked them up or tied them down. Now it's their turn to get even!

### LOOK FOR THESE OTHER TERRIFYING TALES COMING SOON

### MY TEACHER'S A BUG
**77785-1/$3.50 US/$4.50 Can**

### WHERE HAVE ALL THE PARENTS GONE?
**78117-4/$3.50 US/$4.50 Can**